ArtScroll Youth Series®

Rabbi Nosson Scherman / Rabbi Meir Zlotowitz

General Editors

Keeper of

Published by

Mesorah Publications, ltd

the Crown

A novel by **A. Shalom**
Illustrated by **Tova Katz**

FIRST EDITION
First Impression … August 2003

Published and Distributed by
MESORAH PUBLICATIONS, LTD.
4401 Second Avenue / Brooklyn, N.Y 11232

Distributed in Europe by
LEHMANNS
Unit E, Viking Industrial Park
Rolling Mill Road NE32 3DP
Jarow, Tyne & Wear,
England

Distributed in Australia and New Zealand by
GOLDS WORLD OF JUDAICA
3-13 William Street
Balaclava, Melbourne 3183
Victoria Australia

Distributed in Israel by
SIFRIATI / A. GITLER BOOKS
6 Hayarkon Street
Bnei Brak 51127

Distributed in South Africa by
KOLLEL BOOKSHOP
Shop 8A Norwood Hypermarket
Norwood 2196, Johannesburg, South Africa

Typography by CompuScribe at ArtScroll Studios, Ltd.

Printed in the United States of America by Noble Book Press Corp.
Bound by Sefercraft, Quality Bookbinders, Ltd., Brooklyn N.Y. 11232

Over the hills of anger and deceit,

Beyond the waters of arrogance and selfishness,

High above, amidst truth and kindess,

There is my husband,

My favorite Keeper of the Crown.

Author's Note

$\mathcal{S}$ince every story has its birthplace, I would like to begin by thanking my father and mother, who called me creative. Their love and endless support is constant and forever growing.

With deep appreciation, I thank my father-in-law and mother-in-law for their love, for their encouragement, for their strength and for their son.

I am grateful to my grandparents for showing me what is truly important in life. I especially want to thank my grandfather, Ephraim Gurgy Aboudy a"h, who inspired me to write this story.

Credit for the book's production is due to the entire staff of Artscroll/Mesorah. I would like to thank them for their hard work and support, specifically Mrs. Judi Dick and Mrs. Mindy Stern for their encouragement and expert editing, Shmuel Blitz along with Tova Katz for the beautiful illustrations and Avrohom Biderman for skillfully working this book through its many stages. I am again honored for having the opportunity to work with Rabbi Nosson Scherman, whose wise and noble manner has taught me how to be both mindful and respectful of my writing.

I owe a debt of gratitude to Joan Elste, who refuses to settle for anything less than my best.

I am thankful to Rabbi Isaac Dwek, Rabbi Shlomo Diamond, Rabbi Edmund Nahum, Rabbi Shmuel Choueka,

Rabbi Moshe Kuessous and Rabbi David and Chaya Sutton for providing me with the necessary help and guidance to write this story. May G-d bless you with the ability to continue as a strong growing force within our midst.

To Rita Safdiah, her mother, Linda Naftali a"h, Judy Boim and my friends at the Sephardic Archives of the Sephardic Community Center — thank you for your direct hotline to all of my questions and concerns.

I would not have been able to accomplish anything without my family, whom have filled my life with joy and set my standards of love and understanding.

Above all, I would like to express my gratitude to our Father in Heaven, since everything in my life results from His kindness.

CHAPTER ONE

*T*HE BEAT OF QUICK RAPPING ON THE DOOR ECHOED through the *hohsh*.[1] Masuda jumped up, pricking herself with the needle she quickly pulled through her embroidered scarf.

She looked back toward her father, who moved around in his bedroom, before she turned to see who was at the door.

"Don't open it!" Jacob Matalon called as he leaped from his room with a revolver in hand. He pulled Masuda behind him and slid beside the front door.

A gun! She had never seen one this close up before. She knew her father had been in the army, and had even fought in the Great War of 1914. But seeing the gun in his hand, this close up, was different. When he cocked the hammer on the gun, she could do nothing but stand motionless. So motionless, she was afraid to even drop the needle still pinched between her fingers. Her chest rose up and down to the rhythm of her racing heartbeat.

"Yes?" her father asked calmly while pushing aside the window curtain with the tip of his revolver. He turned around to Masuda with his finger over his lips, signaling to remain quiet. Then he tilted his head to see out the window into the courtyard. His eyes narrowed, focused on the view outside the door.

---

1. **hohsh** – (Arabic) a residence with an outdoor courtyard, usually walled on all sides.

"Jacob. It is I, Shaprut! Open the door."

The last rays of the Monday afternoon sun lit up the courtyard. Masuda's father eyed the visitor a little longer before moving. "Yes, it is Shaprut … and he's alone," he said finally. Masuda felt her father's shoulders release as he spoke, relaxing the frightened air around them just a bit as he slid the revolver into the back of his waistband and unlocked the door.

Lately, Masuda had noticed that people seemed especially jittery in Baghdad. Jewish men and women quickened their pace. Everyone was in a hurry to get home. Few sat leisurely outside the teahouses puffing on their *nargeeleh*s.[1] Even her teacher seemed to be looking over her shoulder a little too often. This made sense. There were two deaths this week immediately after *Rosh Hashanah*.[2] One man had been run over outside the *souk*[3] and another had been killed on his way home from synagogue. These things happened every now and then, especially to Jews, but this time it was different.

Iraq changed when it became an independent country four years earlier, in 1932. Before that, the British had ruled Iraq from the time of the Great War, bringing with them modern technology and order. Once the British gave up control, havoc struck. It seemed as if everyone wanted to grab a piece of a country he could call his own. The passing of King Faisal did not make matters better. His son, Prince Ghazi, was appointed to succeed him and all knew he ruled from a position of weakness.

Jacob's assistant stood in the doorway, his lanky figure still too small, in Masuda's opinion, for the trailing turban that sat on his head. His dusty face looked comfortable with his ragged turban and torn sandals.

---

1. **nargeeleh** – (Arabic) a water pipe with a flexible tube for smoking tobacco.
2. **Rosh Hashanah** – (Hebrew) the Jewish New Year.
3. **souk** – (Arabic) a covered marketplace.

Jacob quickly pulled him in and closed the door. The young Arab smiled nervously at the sight of Masuda. Jacob nodded, approving his daughter's presence.

Masuda picked up her embroidery and fastened the needle in the middle. After placing it in a small drawer, she headed toward the kitchen to clear away the dinner dishes.

"It is serious, my friend," Shaprut began. "I am sorry to be the one to tell you …" He looked over at Masuda through the kitchen doorway, fiddling with his worry beads.

"Shaprut." Jacob's unwavering stare locked on his employee. "Tell me what you have found out."

"You have been chosen."

Masuda's father stepped back and wiped his forehead with the palm of his hand.

"Your suspicions were right, Jacob. My uncle confirmed it today. He sits in disbelief with the rest of Iraqi intelligence in headquarters. They are targeting Jewish businessmen, to kill — the wealthier, the better. I'm sorry to say that you were one of their first choices. It is all part of Hikmat Sulayman's plan to take over the country. He has some powerful friends — General Sidqi being the most loyal, and Sidqi is only too happy to do his dirty work for him."

"G-d help us," Jacob said, "The army has been out in full force especially in places of business. So it is true. They are now murdering innocent businessmen!" His voice roared through the *hohsh*.

"Murdering?" Masuda dropped the pot she was scrubbing and ran into the hall.

"Jacob, my uncle told me about their plan to kill you as soon as he was able to confirm it. He feels a deep sense of gratitude to you and your father for supporting our family all these years. He assures us that if we act quickly and leave the country immediately, he will take care of the rest. All will be fine."

Fine? Masuda panicked. How could any of this be fine? Her father was just picked to be murdered, to be *killed*. She hurried into the front room where her father was pacing.

"Fine for me, but not so fine for the next Jewish businessman. Just as long as they —" Jacob said, hesitating at the sight of his daughter. "Masuda." He pointed to his room. "Please ... bring me my glasses."

"But," Masuda started. She did not ask why he would need his reading glasses with no papers to read. She turned around and quietly disappeared.

Her father's glasses were turned over on his bed. She snatched them in her hand and moved slowly toward the doorway, knowing that he did not want them back so soon.

Startled, she jumped back at the sight of a figure moving in the mirror that was fixed on her mother's perfume table. After a few short breaths, Masuda realized that it was her own face staring back at her, searching, hoping for an instant that it was her mother. She yearned to see her mother one last time, to feel her fingertips arranging Masuda's hair, to hear her sweet humming throughout the house. Masuda had cried enough after her mother had passed away. She quickly sighed, hoping to exhale her thoughts all at once.

In the hall, Shaprut wiped the droplets of sweat that formed between the wrinkles of his forehead. "Sulayman, he doesn't care. This Jew or that Jew, it's all the same to him ... as long as he can keep the Jews home in fear long enough for business to stop. Baghdad will shut down and chaos will begin. Then, through General Sidqi, he can bring in the army and get rid of our king, the way he has always wanted to. Sulayman ... may Allah let him die a slow death."

Jacob stood up and pulled a drawstring bag from a drawer in the hall.

"Father?" Masuda said, handing him his glasses. He nodded and pressed them into his front pocket. Then he

handed Masuda the bag, "Pack what you must…just a few things. Until you reach your uncle."

"Jacob, you know I am here to offer my services. Whatever you need. But you must think about traveling alone. You don't want to get your daughter mixed up in any of this."

"Father," Masuda interrupted, "I want go with *you*."

Jacob glanced at his daughter, "I know … but you're only thirteen years old. We must think of your safety first."

"I have arranged for that," Shaprut said. "Your brother Robert, in Aleppo, is the best choice. She will be safe there. Without you, her journey will go unnoticed. Then we can concentrate on your escape. But we must do so immediately. You have been named. If either of you are spotted anywhere in their reach, they will kill you. Let Allah strike them dead first!"

Masuda's father brushed the hair off his forehead and sighed deeply. "Who will escort her?"

"Mrs. Faraj, with Masuda posing as her daughter, is traveling to a family wedding in Aleppo. I worked out the details with her this morning as you suggested. She has the necessary documents and has already agreed to take your daughter."

"Two females traveling alone … what was I thinking?"

"Sending any more protection for her will only call attention to the situation. It will be better this way." Shaprut inched toward the window, glancing nervously outside.

Masuda needed to convince her father. She would much rather take a chance and stay with him. She didn't care how dangerous it was. She saw the way her neighbor, Mrs. Faraj, looked at her. She did not trust her one bit. Shaprut either. He was talking about her as if he knew what was best for her. He didn't even know her.

"You may be right, Shaprut," Jacob said, adjusting the revolver wedged against his back. "But there is still the problem of transportation. How will they get to Aleppo?"

"With Mrs. Faraj's car. It is the best choice. She has driven the route before, and is waiting on Rashid Street as we speak."

CHAPTER TWO

*S*HAPRUT STEPPED ONTO THE STONE PATH, EYEING AND measuring the security on Kambar Ali Street. "All clear. Hurry!"

Jacob Matalon slammed the *hohsh* door shut and grabbed hold of his daughter's hand before following Shaprut. Masuda held on to her father, keeping up with his quick pace. The book in her pocket bounced against her leg. The small *Tanach*[1] was the last thing she had grabbed before leaving her *hohsh* — that, and the overnight bag holding a dress, undergarments and her mother's silver comb. She turned around to take one last look at her home. A group of people passed her *hohsh* on Kambar Ali Street. Could one of them be hoping to kill her father?

"Jacob, I can escort her to Mrs. Faraj myself," Shaprut said.

Jacob Matalon was silent while he kept up his quick stride.

"It is too dangerous for you to be seen right now."

"I am taking no chances with my daughter. This is the way we are going to do it and that is final!"

Masuda turned around. The group down the street she spotted minutes earlier had split apart, leaving two men who steadily continued to trail Masuda, her father and Shaprut. The men stuck out from the crowd in their three-piece suits.

1. **Tanach** – (Hebrew) the twenty-four books of the Bible.

"Father," she whispered, "there are two men behind us."

Jacob swung around. Shaprut pulled him and Masuda forward, his eyes locked on the two men behind. Realizing that they were noticed, the men pretended to be engaged in conversation with an old beggar at the side of the road.

"Shaprut," Jacob whispered. He spied the open alley to their right and tugged Masuda's hand. "Run, Masuda!" he told his daughter just before he sprinted down the alley.

Masuda grabbed onto her father as they dashed down the winding passage, followed closely by Shaprut. She could feel the bag twisting in her hand. At once the strap broke and the bag fell to the ground.

Her clothes and her mother's comb! She reached to get it.

"Leave it!" Shaprut demanded, pushing her ahead.

The cape buttoned at her neck flapped against her shoulders. Her shoes beat against the rocky ground. She took another quick glance behind. Although she could not see the men following them in the mazed alley, she could hear their voices echoing down the stone path. "Down that way! He's with his daughter!"

Sudden noises from the Hanoon Market pierced the air. As they pushed on, the sounds of squawking animals mixed with bickering buyers and merchants from Baghdad's *souk* rose clearly.

Jacob led the way. "The copper market will let us out on Rashid," he whispered to Shaprut.

After the next curve they disappeared under the old canopied *souk* of Baghdad, halted by the crowds in their way.

The familiar colors, sounds and scents of the *souk* now seemed unfamiliar to Masuda. No longer a comfort to her memory, they were now intrusions. The crimson scarves, the turquoise and jade silver, the bargaining and shouting that preceded each sale, the mounds of roasted pumpkin

seeds, almonds and pistachio nuts, and the sturdy scent of rosewater which could even mask the foul odor of the Bedouin women were now all banded together in one strange puzzle, a puzzle which included the plot to murder her father.

Each sound pushed her farther away from the life she knew. She looked around as if looking from the outside in like a stranger, foreign to the familiar life she had once lived.

A toothless woman dangled a pearl necklace before Masuda's eyes. Masuda jumped suddenly and then looked away nervously, trying to catch her breath.

"It's all right. I am here," her father told her.

"Keep going," urged Shaprut.

They hurried on, weaving through the market. Her father pushed by the fat bellies and cupped hands of beggars who cluttered their path. "Gib chai! Bring tea!" a merchant yelled to his young helper as he spotted a promising sale.

Aromas of cumin and Turkish coffee hit Masuda's nose. Fried mutton and buffalo grease hung in the air. Sweat dripped down the back of her neck as she darted with her father and Shaprut through the streaks of light that managed to shine through the covered market.

Children blocked their way, grouping around a bunch of tourists in the marketplace. They flashed their eager smiles at the foreigners, insisting on carrying their baskets. Acting as guides for these strangers, the children then escorted the tourists to their desired crafts, hoping to collect a cut from the selected vendors.

"Coming through," yelled Shaprut, nudging Masuda and Jacob forward.

Jacob looked past Shaprut, eyeing the crowds.

"Not to worry," Shaprut said. "We have lost them, for now."

Feeew! An iron weight flew by, barely an inch from Masuda's ear. Jacob pushed Masuda aside as a fight broke out at a fruit and vegetable stall. One man grabbed the vendor, twisting the front of his robe in his fist and then spit down on the scale. Children pounced on the ground to gather the tomatoes and okra that bounced at their feet.

"You cheated me!" the man hollered at the vendor.

"I swear by the holy prophet ..." the vendor choked out the words as the other man pinned him against the wall. "This weight is at least a kilo[1] ... see," he said, taking off the weight and tossing another kilo weight onto the scale. He then pointed to the rickety scales, as the scale holding the weight sat almost even beside the scale holding the produce. "Look, I cheat myself. I give you extra. I cheat myseeeelf!" the vendor screeched as the man lifted him above the ground by his throat.

Masuda could hardly see where she was going. Her father pulled her through the crowds. She twitched as the merchants raised their voices and she cringed at their unfamiliar faces, wondering if there was even one who might recognize her father.

"Master Matalon!" someone bellowed behind them.

Masuda's heart dropped.

Shaprut reached for his gun.

Jacob spun around. The friendly merchant called him again, "Jacob! I thought it was you! I close up soon. How about a drink at the café?"

"Yes, Matlub! Later!" Jacob called back over the bobbing heads.

Because her father held her so tightly, Masuda's hand was red and raw by the time they reached the copper market, identified by its steady pounding rhythm. Sweat glistened on the dark faces of men hunched over their metal pots, as they hammered fiercely, each one's deafening beat

---

1. **kilo** – 2.2 pounds.

rising above the other. Masuda, her father and Shaprut whisked by the little boys who worked the bellows, helping their fathers keep the fires hot enough to soften the metal. Masuda felt faint at the stench of cow chips burning in the glowing fires.

Jacob turned to his daughter suddenly before exiting the copper market. He rested his hands on her shoulders, peering into her eyes. "Masuda. You are on your own now." He looked up, skimming the crowds. "I will meet you at Uncle Robert's house in Aleppo as soon as I am able to. You have the money I gave you?"

"Yes, Father." She tugged at the pocket in her dress.

"G-d be with you," he said, his voice almost a whisper.

Masuda clung to Jacob, holding him tight. "What about you, Father?"

"I will be fine. You will see."

Shaprut leaned against Jacob. "Hurry! There is no time!"

Outside the *souk*, Jacob gazed into the distance, pushing Masuda past the goats and chickens that roamed Rashid Street.

Shaprut tapped Jacob's arm and nodded in the direction of the black automobile ahead. A woman sat behind the wheel in the front seat.

"Mrs. Faraj," Shaprut said. "This is as far as we should go."

"It's time, Masuda."

Masuda stood before her father. Tears streamed down her face. Her mind raced, trying to fit her entire life into this one moment. She kissed her father's hand and brushed it against her cheek. "I love you, Father," was all she could say before running to the car.

CHAPTER THREE

THE BLACK AUTOMOBILE SPED ALONG THE WINDING road on Tuesday morning, spinning crushed rock off its dusty tires. The sudden motion jerked Masuda awake. Even in her sleep, she gripped the handle at her side and held herself close to the passenger door so as not to lean anywhere in the direction of Mrs. Faraj. Masuda knew that she was in her neighbor's hands now. She had to keep to herself, stay out of trouble. She also knew that the Syrian mountains were just several hours away but still far from her Uncle Robert in Aleppo, and so far from safety. She would do nothing to upset their plans.

Although they had been traveling in the car since the night before, Masuda had not really fallen asleep until a few hours ago, when the first rays of sun announced the new morning. And while she thought that sleep might help wash away her deepest fears, she still felt the knot in her stomach, leftover from their escape.

The October air gave no relief to the desert weather. Hot and sandy, she could not figure out which was more uncomfortable — to be out there in the sun, or to be in the car with a limited supply of the grimy air rushing through the small opening of the window. And whatever decent air was left, she was sure Mrs. Faraj had gotten to it first.

The afternoon sun, without so much as a cloud interrupting its heated rays, beat through the windshield. The hot, sticky package of dates was the only thing separating Mrs. Faraj from Masuda. That and bread were all they had to eat for their journey to Aleppo. The water jug nestled in the back seat. Driving through the desert, she was glad they had plenty of water. At least enough to last until the next stop.

Masuda arched her back, stretching her stiff muscles. Something dug into her thigh. She had felt it while she was sleeping. She reached down to touch her pocket and remembered. It was the book in her pocket. More than just a book, it was the entire twenty-four books of the *Torah* packed in one small volume. The letters of the *Tanach* were so small one could hardly read them. She adjusted it in her pocket, making sure Mrs. Faraj would not see. She was not certain whether it would be proper for her, posing as an Armenian, to be holding such a thing, and she did not want to find out for sure.

When she was born, her father had tucked this book into the side of her crib. There was an inscription on the first page that read, *My dear Masuda, G-d has blessed you. Keep His words with you always.* Sometimes she just opened the book and looked at the inscription for a long time. It was the only thing her father had written to her.

Aside from the folded *fils*[1] in her dress, the *Tanach* was also the only thing that survived her escape. Her bag that she had dropped during their flight was probably in the hands of the Iraqi Intelligence. She was thankful that there was nothing in there that could help them locate her father, and she hoped that by now, they had given up their search.

A scorpion scampered behind a rock, missing the speeding tire by a good meter.[2] Masuda looked out the window at the ancient caravan route that had linked traders of Aleppo

---

1. **fils** – Iraqi currency circa 1935.
2. **meter** – a basic unit of measure in the metric system equal to 39.3701 inches or 3.25 feet.

with their buyers in Baghdad. Bedouin families poked at the sheep outside their tents.

"Some milk?" a Bedouin woman called from outside the tent as she stood up at the sight of the automobile passing by. Masuda was close enough to notice her black teeth, evidence of the Bedouin diet, which consisted mostly of dried dates.

Masuda pushed her loose black curls off her face and fastened them with her hairclip. Her round eyes gazed past the yellowish-white haze into the dry stillness. This woman's ancestors had been pitching tents in these deserts for thousands of years. How simple life must have been for them, she thought. How different from today.

She remembered the last conversation she had had with her father. "It will be better this way, safer for you with Uncle Robert in Aleppo," he had tried to convince her.

"Please, Father! Take me with you. I won't be any trouble," she had said, giving in to her tears. "I don't want to be away from you."

·   "Your uncle is expecting you and your cousins are, too."

"But what will happen to you? They want to kill you!"

"Don't worry about me. Hashem will take care of me. Besides ..." Jacob paused at the sound of his voice cracking in his throat, "I will come for you as soon as I can."

"I miss you already, Father," Masuda said, tears covering her face.

Now in the car, she thought of that moment when her father had hugged her. She prayed it wouldn't be the last.

Mrs. Faraj drove on. Her double chin wiggled as she chewed on sunflower seeds, spitting out the shells. Probably leftovers from last night, thought Masuda.

When her neighbor turned toward her, Masuda looked away, staring out the window. "So, you understand that you must not say anything," Mrs. Faraj said. "You are my daughter and we are going to visit my niece, your cousin, in

Aleppo for her wedding. You will be changing there, where your party dress is waiting."

"Yes, I remember." Masuda nodded.

"You know, in Aleppo the people don't call their city by that name. It's Halab to everyone who lives there. It has always been Halab."

Masuda raised her eyebrows and nodded at the piece of information, which she already knew. Mrs. Faraj fingered her beaded necklace with one hand, while steering the car with the other. Masuda noticed her hair, uncovered, but neatly pulled back into a sort of a bun. Mrs. Faraj turned to her and smiled as she stuck her pinky nail between her two gold teeth to loosen a wedged shell.

For the rest of the day, the only activities were stopping to use the bathroom, or hole in the ground, at the IPC Petroleum stop, refilling the water jug and eating Mrs. Faraj's hot, grimy dates. Maybe she would sleep again after all.

CHAPTER FOUR

THE EVENING SUN APPROACHED THE HORIZON. Masuda awoke, pulling her cape over her shoulders. The nights in the desert grew cold just as quickly as the days grew hot.

"This is it," Mrs. Faraj whispered beside her.

Masuda sat up. The car slowed down as it approached the next patrol checkpoint. Masuda knew that this was the Iraqi border patrol because she could see the Syrian mountains looming in the distance. She spotted two guards in army uniform sharing a cigarette.

Masuda's heart sank. Why hadn't she realized it before? Her Arabic had a Jewish slant to it, different from Mrs. Faraj. What would she say if they spoke to her? She stared at the guards, trying to act natural. It was too late to pretend that she was sleeping. They had already seen her awake. Oh, why did she have to wake up! Now they would know. As soon as she spoke, they would know everything.

The guard lifted his hand to stop the automobile. Mrs. Faraj rolled the car over to him and lowered her window, painting on a smile that seemed to stretch from one ear to the next. "*Masa il khehr!* Good evening!" she called out her window.

One of the guards stepped right up to her window. "Where are you going?" he asked in perfect English.

Masuda started breathing again. What a relief. A British officer. They could never tell the difference between the Arabic of a Jew and the Arabic of a Muslim. She had forgotten that a small British presence still remained in Iraq, even after Britain officially pulled out its forces four years earlier.

Mrs. Faraj motioned to Masuda. "We are on our way to a family wedding in Aleppo."

The guard lifted his lit cigarette and sucked in a breath. Smoke poured out steadily from his nostrils. "That is quite a drive you have." He poked his head through the window. "And she is ..."

"My daughter," Mrs. Faraj answered as she straightened her papers and handed them to the guard.

He sifted through them. His stare shifted from Masuda to Mrs. Faraj and back to the documents.

Masuda smiled quietly. Mrs. Faraj tapped her foot nervously. The guard returned the papers to Mrs. Faraj and stepped away from the car before signaling to the other officer to open the gate.

Although she did not speak one word to the guard, Masuda sensed that things were going her way. This feeling stayed with her as they crossed the border into Syria, passing the small town of Abu Kemal. And here, she would have a chance to brush up on her French. Although Britain had pulled out of Iraq, France held tight to Syria and Lebanon, another result of the Great War. French was the main language spoken in Syria. Even the schools were subject to this. When Masuda's cousin spoke to his teacher in Arabic, he had to pay for it, with the only coin he held in his pocket.

Only seven more hours of traveling until she reached her Uncle Robert in Aleppo. There was just one small delay. They would spend the night at Mrs. Faraj's brother, in Dier al-Zor, about 95 kilometers[1] north of Abu Kemal. This was

---

1. **kilometer** – one thousand meters, 3,280.84 feet or .6214 miles.

part of the plan from the start. But Masuda didn't care. They were out of Iraq and out of danger. Maybe she would even be able to sleep on a real mattress.

She thought about her father and hoped he had escaped safely just as she had. But what if he didn't? She wasn't going to think about that. Things were going her way and everything was going to be fine, just as her father had said it would.

Hours later they arrived at the house of Mrs. Faraj's brother. Masuda stepped out of the car and into the darkness. She could hardly stand. Her wobbly legs almost buckled under her weight. Mrs. Faraj fussed with a handkerchief to make herself look presentable. Masuda couldn't imagine her looking much different.

The house stood against the blackness of the night sky on the northern bank of the Euphrates River. She remembered hearing a story that had taken place near there. Her father had told her about the Tower of Babel and how its tall structure had collapsed. They had driven by the Euphrates on her last visit to Aleppo, when she was ten. She looked over the tall grass now, where the water hit the bank. Her eyes tried to follow the narrow river down toward Iraq where her father once pointed out the sight. "You see that mountain over there?" he had said, pointing to the ruins of the Tower of Babel piled high.

But the moon barely offered any light. Only enough to take her eyes down the river as far as a nearby house, two cotton fields away.

Howling wild dogs pierced the nighttime music of the insects, which blanketed the rich vegetation along the river. Masuda shivered. What was she doing out here in the middle of the wilderness?

Mrs. Faraj slammed the car door, beckoning Masuda to follow. They walked up the dirt path toward the house. Before they reached the steps, a boy flung open the front door. The light from inside lit their way. His raspy voice called out, "Auntie! It's Auntie!" He skipped down the front steps and stopped at the sight of Masuda.

"Jamil, is that you?" Mrs. Faraj asked him. "When did you grow taller than me?"

The boy reached for the bag in Mrs. Faraj's grip.

"I can carry it myself," Mrs. Faraj said, shaking his hand off the strap. "Parasite, that nephew of mine," she added after he walked off. Then she turned to Masuda, "Come meet my brother, the baker."

"Father, its Auntie!" Jamil called to his father standing in the doorway. "She brought a girl," he said quietly, although Masuda was still able to hear his words.

"I can see that. Woman!" the baker called to his wife inside the house.

A small woman shuffled to the doorway with a basket in her arms. She poked her head through the doorway and grunted at the sight of Mrs. Faraj before returning to her chores.

Masuda followed Mrs. Faraj inside. There, the baker's wife sat the basket of laundry on her hip while she tossed a loaf of bread on the table. Then she brought a small dish, which she splashed with oil.

"Let's sit," Mrs. Faraj motioned to Masuda, who stood beside her. There were no chairs and no sofas. Masuda understood that *sit* meant sitting on the woven rug that covered the floor along one side of the room, especially after she noticed the pillows lined up against the wall for extra comfort. She sat down next to Mrs. Faraj, looking up at the bright blue tapestry hanging overhead almost concealing the hole in the wall.

"This girl I brought with me," she said, displaying Masuda. "I was hired to escort her to Damascus. Her name is … Hagar," she said finally.

Masuda turned to Mrs. Faraj with a questioning look.

She had it all wrong. Her name was not Hagar and they were definitely not traveling to Damascus.

Mrs. Faraj's eyes kept Masuda from speaking. Just one look told Masuda that Mrs. Faraj knew exactly what she was saying and why. It was for her own protection and Mrs. Faraj was right, thought Masuda. It would be better this way. No one had to know who she was or where she was going.

Mrs. Faraj introduced the dark man to Masuda as her brother.

"There is something for you to eat … on the table," Mrs. Faraj offered Masuda. "The bread should be good. My brother brings it home from his shop, fresh every day."

"No, thank you," said Masuda. She stood up from the rug on the floor. "But if there is a little water, I would like to wash my hands."

"Jamil!" the baker called to his son.

Jamil stood up in the corner, where he was twisting a piece of straw into a finger ring. "I'll do it," he answered, as he grabbed the empty clay jug. The red figure drawn on the jug seemed to dance with him as he opened the front door and flew out into the night.

The baker's wife came up behind Masuda with an empty basin and a cotton cloth. "You can use these to wash up. If you want some privacy, you may use Jamil's room, over there behind the curtain." She pointed down the hall. Then she added softly, "I'm sure Jamil won't mind."

As if he just heard his name, Jamil stormed through the door, suddenly slowing his pace as he skidded toward Masuda. He set the pitcher down in front of her.

Masuda nodded with a half smile and filled the basin, studying the drawing of the woman on the pitcher. It was more like a painted figure, filled in with some sort of red color that had since dried and flaked off. But the eyes of the woman, black and awkward, seemed to stare right at her.

Masuda looked away, shaking off the chill that had traveled up her back.

"Down that way, child…at the end of the hall," the baker's wife said.

Masuda walked down the hall, fighting the stares coming her way.

The only thing defining Jamil's room was a tattered curtain that hung from a pole and reached from one side of the narrow hall to the other. Without it, his room was just the end of the hall. She set the basin down on the floor and pulled the curtain across. In the room stood a mattress leaning against the wall. On top of the mattress was a cotton robe tangled with a pair of sandals. Dust laced the frame of a small window.

Masuda dipped the cloth into the basin and wrung it out. The curtain did not do much to quiet their voices.

"How much money?" the baker asked.

"Shhh," Masuda could hear Mrs. Faraj say. "He promised me the rest of the money once I finish the job and return to Baghdad."

"And what makes you so sure her father will pay, once the job is already done?"

"I have been able to trust her father before. There is no reason to doubt him now."

Masuda ran the cold cloth over her sandy face. They were talking about her and her father. Her skin shivered not only from the cold water. She missed her father and her loneliness seemed to penetrate straight into her bones.

The baker's wife cleared her throat. "This girl may be suitable for Jamil. And I think—"

"No!" Mrs. Faraj answered firmly.

Masuda froze. She stared at the curtain, unable to move.

"Father?" the small woman called her husband. "You know it is time for us to find the boy a wife. And why are you being so protective anyway?" she snapped at Mrs. Faraj. "It's not like you have been given all kinds of money to be her guardian. I wonder if you will ever see the rest of the money you were promised."

"Woman, that is enough!" bellowed the baker at his wife.

Masuda shifted slightly, catching a glimpse of them. Mrs. Faraj dipped a piece of bread into the oil and popped it into her mouth. "It doesn't matter what anyone thinks," she said, chewing. "I gave my word that I would bring this girl safely to Damascus and that is exactly what I am going to do!" She reached down behind the pillow and pulled on her bag. Caught on a nail in the floor, the bag stayed firm. "Now if you'll ex—cuse—me," she said, in between tugs. "I will … Oooh … Ahhh!" she yelled out in pain.

Masuda stepped out from behind the curtain to find Mrs. Faraj hunched over with her bag dangling from her hanging arm. "It's my back. No one touch me!" she said, warding them off with her free hand.

"I can straighten you out. Let me help you." The baker tried to approach her.

Masuda rushed down the hall. Jamil stepped in closer.

"I remember how you helped me the last time. I was in bed for a whole week."

"Well, you can't be any worse than the way you look now. Here, let me help you," he said taking hold of his sister's arm.

"I'm warning you, brother. You had better be real gentle…and make sure that lanky son of yours stays clear away, you hear me? Real gentle or I'll beat you the way Mama did when we were little."

"Just stand still. I think I have it," the baker said, adjusting the position of his hands around her arms and her back.

With a sudden movement, he pulled his arms up and Mrs. Faraj with him.

"Ouuch!" she screamed as her back snapped back into

place. Masuda wondered whether her scream was loud enough for the neighbors, two cotton fields away, to hear.

Mrs. Faraj stood as stiff as a board. Everyone waited for her response.

"Well now you did it!" she called to her brother without moving her head. "You straightened me out, but I can't move. I'm afraid to even take a step."

Masuda came to her side. "Can I help you lie down?"

"Not on the rug," the baker said. "She'll never be able to bend that low. Woman!" he yelled to his wife. "Give her my bed. This way, you can watch her during the night to see if she needs help. I have to be at the bakery most of the night anyway. It won't be a problem finding a soft sack of flour to sleep on if I get tired."

Masuda stood at one side of Mrs. Faraj, while the dark man stood at the other. Mrs. Faraj moaned as they eased her onto the bed in the baker's bedroom. Jamil's mother came in to remove Mrs. Faraj's shoes and to cover her with a blanket.

"Hagar," Mrs. Faraj pulled Masuda close, straining to speak. "Please bring me my bag."

Masuda found Mrs. Faraj's bag just where she had left it. As she lifted it off the floor, a key fell out. Masuda reached to pick it up and turned it over in her hand. It was the key to the car. Something told her to hold onto it. It was just a feeling. She didn't know where this feeling came from. It just popped into her thoughts. Without realizing why, she slipped the key into her dress pocket before returning to Mrs. Faraj.

"Your bag," Masuda said quietly when she returned.

"Hagar?" Mrs. Faraj opened her eyes.

"Yes, I am here," Masuda said.

"I know you are expecting me to take you to your uncle. But in my condition, it will take at least a week, maybe ten days. Do not worry, child. You are safe now. No one will come for you. As soon as I can walk, we will set out for

Aleppo. Even if I am unable to drive, we will find a way to get there. We can take the train," Mrs. Faraj whispered, squeezing her eyes in pain. "I know there is a station about three kilometers north of here. The train leaves for Aleppo twice a day, at midnight and in the morning. We will plan for that as soon as I am able. But you are safe now...safe," Mrs. Faraj repeated before drifting off to sleep.

Masuda closed the door gently and rubbed her skirts. When she turned around, she came face to face with the baker's wife, smiling awkwardly.

CHAPTER FIVE

*T*HANKFUL FOR THE QUIET AND YET FEARFUL OF what it might bring, Masuda curled up on the mattress in Jamil's room, unable to sleep. Just thirty minutes earlier, while she sat in this room removing her shoes, the curtain flapped. Her head sprang up to find two bare feet darting by. Now, Jamil slept soundly on a row of pillows down the hall.

She struggled to organize her thoughts and tried to somehow make sense of all that had happened and where all of this would take her. When she was able to push away her concerns about the baker's wife, Masuda thought about her last conversation with Mrs. Faraj, right after she had slipped the car key into her pocket. Mrs. Faraj tried to assure Masuda that she was safe. But why did she tell her about the train and exactly when it left for Aleppo? Mrs. Faraj had no idea if they would be taking a train, and anyway, that was at least a week away.

The plan now was to stay here for a week or longer and wait, wait for Mrs. Faraj to recover so that they could drive to Aleppo. But Masuda was thirteen years old and old enough to think for herself! If only she knew how to drive a car! If only she knew the way to Aleppo, she would go herself. She didn't care about what anyone else would think, even if it was unheard of for any respectable girl to be traveling alone.

She rolled over onto her stomach and hit something on the floor with her hand. It was Jamil's shoe. She instinctively pushed it away, shoving it into the corner with the rest of his things. Then she looked over at the brown leather sandal, thankful that Jamil was not in it. How was she ever going to survive living with these people for a whole week, maybe more? It would be Shabbat in three days. What's more, Yom Kippur[1] falls on this Shabbat. Where was she going to get a wick that was long enough to light the candles? How would she be able to fast without a *seuda*?[2] She never had to think about these things before. She had had her father to take care of everything.

She couldn't stay here. The walls around her seemed to be closing in. What would stop Jamil from walking in on her, or worse, what would stop them from kidnapping her to serve as a wife to Jamil? Surely Mrs. Faraj would protest the way she had done before, but she was bedridden. What would become of her, and when would they leave for Aleppo, if ever? There must be a way to get to her uncle. What would her father do if he were here?

Masuda sat up suddenly as an idea shot through her thoughts. Her round eyes darted from side to side. It was a plan that just might work, she thought. And the best part was that she didn't need Mrs. Faraj. She didn't even need to know how to drive!

---

1. **Yom Kippur** – (Hebrew) the Day of Atonement.
2. **seuda** – (Hebrew) meal

CHAPTER SIX

*M*ASUDA SAT ON THE MATTRESS, HAVING SECOND thoughts. She was all ready. She tied the ends of her skirts in a knot between her legs. Over her dress, she wore Jamil's robe that she found tangled in the corner beside her mattress. The sandals, which she assumed were his as well, were a little too big. She had to fasten the strap on the tightest hole just so that they wouldn't fall off. She tied her hair in a double loop at the back of her head. Over it, she draped a white *kaffiyeh*,[1] which was also Jamil's. She fastened it with a black corded crown, called an *agal*. She had seen Shaprut wear his head-covering this way in Baghdad.

No one would know who she was. Disguised as a boy, she would have a better chance of traveling unnoticed and unharmed.

Masuda wished she had a timepiece to know exactly what time it was. Mrs. Faraj said that the train station was about three kilometers north of here. Mapping out a clear path in her mind, she figured that was about a twenty-minute walk. If the train was leaving for Aleppo at midnight, that did not leave her much time. She remembered Mrs. Faraj pulling out her timepiece before they drove up to her brother's house. It was nine o'clock then. She figured it was about eleven–thirty now. There was no time to lose.

---

1. **kaffiyeh** – (Arabic) an Arab headdress for men held in place by an *agal*.

She needed to get past Jamil. She opened the curtain and peeked down the hall. Darkness filled the small house. It was a heavy darkness, weighed down by her own fears. She tried to picture the path to the door. Bumping into anything was a sure way to alert everyone to her escape.

When she stood, the key shifted in her pocket and she made a mental note to place it by the front door before leaving.

She inched her way down the hall with her hand grazing the wall. She passed the baker's bedroom door, hearing the sound of a bed frame hit the wall as someone tossed in her sleep. Only now did she realize just how small the house was.

Slowly she stepped toward the front door. She could hear Jamil in the corner, snoring loudly. A thin stream of moonlight shone through the small window on his bare feet, which hung over a pillow against the wall. Her heart pounded so fast, she was afraid to even breathe.

She was almost there. She pushed down on the door handle and pulled the front door open just wide enough to be able to slip out. Then she closed it gently, but not before she heard Jamil pop up from the sofa and whisper, "Who's there?"

Masuda flew down the steps, losing all sense of caution. She twisted from side to side, making certain she knew which way was north. Since they were on the northern bank of the Euphrates River, north meant away from the river. As she turned in that direction, she suddenly heard the door of the house creak open. She crouched behind the car, watching from the front fender. There in the doorway stood Jamil, peering into the darkness.

He waddled down the steps, stopping just before the last one.

Masuda held her breath and focused her gaze on the small pebbles that sprayed the dirt path, hoping that they would keep his bare feet from taking another step.

If he discovered her she would never catch the train to Aleppo. Besides that, she feared for her life, not knowing how they would react to her attempting to leave. Mrs. Faraj was the only one who seemed sympathetic to her. But that wouldn't mean much after she found out that Masuda had betrayed her.

Jamil stepped back into the house and closed the door. Masuda let out a short breath. Then fear grabbed her once again as she imagined Jamil returning to the hallway and noticing the curtain to his room pushed aside. The mattress would be visible from the opening and he would know that she was gone. She stared at the door. If she waited any longer she would miss her train. Should she run now? Even if Jamil had no shoes on, she could never outrun him to the station once he discovered she was missing. It was too far. He would catch up with her. She had no doubt.

Remembering that she had not left the key for Mrs. Faraj, she opened the door to the car and crawled in, carefully clicking the door closed. Then she slid into the driver's seat and reached into the pocket of her dress. She could feel the hard metal deep in her pocket, wedged into the corner of the bottom seam. Finally she yanked it out and stuck the small edge into the ignition hole. Now what?

She pressed down on the clutch pedal the way she had seen Mrs. Faraj do and turned the key to the right.

The motor coughed to the beat of loud chucking and puffing. Finally it caught and she could feel the engine rumbling. She pressed on the floor with her right foot, reaching for the gas pedal while still keeping her left foot down on the clutch. Her foot tapped the brake instead and she pushed down on the pedal. Nothing happened. She tried again, harder this time, but all it did was stiffen the feel of any movement of the car.

She looked up in panic. "Please, Hashem! Help me!"

Glancing back through the window, she could see Jamil

running toward her. His mother followed behind him with a lantern, waving her hand in the air trying to flag her down.

In a panic, Masuda lifted her foot off the clutch a few inches and the car lunged forward. She immediately slammed her foot down.

Jamil chuckled. His mother shrieked.

I'm doing something wrong, Masuda thought. She remembered watching Mrs. Faraj when she drove the car. Mrs. Faraj didn't use the clutch pedal all the time.

Masuda tried again. She took her foot off the clutch and pressed down on the gas. The car surged forward and again she slammed the clutch pedal to the floor.

Jamil and his mother were almost upon her now, less than a meter from the car. Masuda closed her eyes and pressed down hard on the gas pedal while lifting her foot off the clutch at the same time. The car burst ahead, speeding down the hill in first gear and sailing across the field.

After glancing about once more, she saw Jamil and his mother in the light of the lantern. At least she had left two fils on the windowsill of his room, which was more than enough money to replace his robe and worn sandals.

CHAPTER SEVEN

*M*ASUDA LEANED HER FOREHEAD AGAINST THE WINDOW of the train as it slowly pulled out of the station.

"To Beirut!" the conductor called out to each of the passengers boarding the train.

Masuda glanced out the window to the spot where she had left Mrs. Faraj's automobile. Just moments ago, she had tossed the keys onto the driver's seat before running to catch the train. She knew that Mrs. Faraj would search the station for the car. After all, traveling to Aleppo by train was her idea.

The train whistled, echoing into the night. Masuda adjusted her headdress. She had to stick to her story, posing as a boy. She slouched over and turned to face the window, hoping to avoid any conversation. It wasn't going to be that difficult, she thought. The train was practically empty. Aside from the man two rows ahead who arranged his crates of chickens, only a small cat brushed by Masuda, slithering down the narrow aisle.

Framing the window was a band of dirt. Masuda ran her finger over it. It felt wet and slippery, more like grease than dirt. She rubbed it between her fingers. Then she looked around to make sure no one was looking while she smeared the grease across her forehead and over the rest of her face. At least now her face matched her disguise.

Masuda tried with difficulty to smile at the idea of completing her false identity. Her head pounded and her eyes saw spotty black wherever she turned. It was a miracle that she had reached the station in one piece, she thought. At first she couldn't find the switch for the car's headlights. With only the moon to guide her, she managed to skirt around the houses that dotted the fields. It was a good thing she found the switch before she arrived at the station, otherwise she would have smashed into the rails at 50 kilometers per hour.

Her escape drove her thoughts, and her mind and body were as one — on watch and alert for any predators. She gazed anxiously out the window, almost afraid that she would see Jamil and his family coming to get her.

The train picked up speed, vibrating and rumbling along its course. Masuda let her breath out slowly, straightening in her seat. She stopped herself from looking over her shoulder once more. She could forget now about Mrs. Faraj's family. They were gone.

She was leaving Dier al-Zor, and nothing would stop her. She sat up, staring out the window, hoping to catch a glimpse of the cities whizzing by. This was her future and she was not going to dwell on the past. The train churned parallel to the Euphrates River. Dier al-Zor, Halebiye, Raqqa, Qal'at Jabar, Meskineh, Zabed, Mullaq and Sifreh were all on the way to Aleppo. Some were ancient cities, dating back to biblical times. She nervously scraped Jamil's sandals along the floor and tried to think about the different tales surrounding these cities. Although Syria had many conquerors, including the Greeks, Romans, Arabs, Crusaders, Ottoman Turks and the twentieth century French, Masuda focused on the Syria that existed during the days of King Solomon — when the first *Beit Hamikdash*[1] towered over Jerusalem and the Name of Hashem rang clear. And with that thought, her eyelids became heavy and she dozed off.

---

1. **Beit Hamikdash** – (Hebrew) the Holy Temple.

CHAPTER EIGHT

*T*HE FAINT STEADY SOUND OF A BABY CRYING SHOOK Masuda from a deep sleep. She jumped up suddenly and opened her eyes in a panic, looking wildly around her. Who were all these people? Did she miss her stop? But then she realized it was still dark outside. If the train had reached Aleppo, it would be morning.

She rubbed her eyes. Worry dug deep into her thoughts as the train passed its halfway mark to Aleppo. What was she thinking, to ride alone on a train, in the middle of the night? Even if she arrived safely in Aleppo, where would she go? How would she find her uncle? She knew he lived in Aleppo, but where exactly?

Was she crazy to think that she would be any safer here, wandering around in Syria, than with Mrs. Faraj and her family? At least there she had food, water and a car.

Yesterday's events rushed through her mind — hearing the news of the plot to kill her father, running through the *souk*, driving through the desert, stopping with Mrs. Faraj at her brother's house. She was supposed to wait for Mrs. Faraj. Once she was well, they would go to Aleppo together as planned.

But Masuda couldn't wait. Imagine ten days at the mercy of Mrs. Faraj's family. Would she have been able to trust them? She wasn't willing to take that chance.

Yes. She had made the right decision. It had to be the

right one. But one thing still bothered her — the thing that caused her to jump up in the first place. If the train had not yet reached Aleppo, then why were there so many new passengers? She slid her way out of the bench, trying to catch sight of the conductor. Maybe the train had made a stop at another city on the way. It was possible. She had been sleeping for a long time.

The man with the chickens was still on board. She stepped over one of his crates to get down the aisle. When she did that, the man, who smelled like a farm animal on a hot day, bellowed at her in his most vulgar Arabic.

"Sorry," Masuda said after leaping ahead. Jamil's oversized sandals, which hung off her heels, slapped the floor with each step she took.

Next to the man with the chickens was a mother cradling her baby. It was still crying, bundled up and cradled in its mother's arms, but still crying. It was a wonder that the man sitting directly in front of the baby was sound asleep.

The train consisted of a number of cars. The few cars in the front were reserved for passengers while the back cars were loaded with grain and cattle. Masuda's car was at the head of the train. She continued walking, hoping to get some information from the conductor.

The conductor's cubicle was empty. Masuda walked back toward her seat. As she walked past the sleepy man, she noticed a black hat that had fallen onto the floor by his foot. The European Jews dressed that way, she thought. She had seen photographs from newspaper articles and was almost certain. She reached for the hat and stretched it out to him, hoping that he would wake up. The train car swung and swayed causing Masuda to hit the rabbi in his chin with the brim of the hat.

"Huh!" he jumped up suddenly, opening his eyes.

"Rabbi, you dropped this," Masuda said, offering him his hat. "Can I ask you —?"

The rabbi snatched his hat from her grip quickly as she started to speak and closed his eyes before settling into his sleep.

Masuda stepped back, startled by the response she had never expected from a rabbi, even if she was dressed like an Arab.

On the way back to her seat, she passed the man with the chickens. He seemed at home in his surroundings and it looked as if he had made this trip before. "Halab?" she asked in her deepest voice.

The man grunted without disturbing his frowning face.

"Halab?" asked the woman whose baby was still crying, "In two hours, boy. Go back to sleep."

It took Masuda a minute to realize that the woman was speaking to her, as if Masuda were an Arab boy like any other, whose long robe touched the tip of his sandals and whose headdress flapped around his smooth, soft face. *Boy,* the woman had called her.

CHAPTER NINE

M ASUDA SHADED HER EYES FROM THE MORNING SUN AS she stepped off the train from Dier al-Zor. She pushed past the rest of the passengers, hoping to speak to the rabbi she had startled on the train. The man with the chickens threw his arm into the air and hollered to his friend with a pushcart who stood waiting for him by the side of the train. The woman with the baby walked slowly toward the town, holding her child close. The rabbi was nowhere in sight. Where could he be?

Masuda took a deep breath and tried to exhale her fears. Adjusting her agal, she hesitantly looked ahead at the sandy road of Aleppo. The train stood on barren land, at least a few hundred meters from the town. There, in town, she would find someone else to lead her to her uncle. Even though the city was mostly Muslim, she could tell the difference between a Muslim and a Jew. The Muslims were browner, with wide jaws and noses shaped like the old Arab sword, short and curved. The Jews, except for the rabbis, mostly wore suits and ties, at least in Baghdad. And she figured life in Syria wasn't much different.

With no better idea in mind, Masuda followed the crowd south to the town of Djamiliyeh.[1] She stepped around a big pink rock, careful not to disturb the camouflaged lizard resting on top.

---

1. **Djamiliyeh** – (Arabic) a town in Aleppo.

An old man smacked the side of his pushcart, coaxing one of the wooden slats back into place. He looked up at Masuda, revealing a toothless mouth. "Cheese?"

Although her empty stomach grumbled at the sight of the food, Masuda hesitated. It was not the hovering flies that bothered her. How could she know if the cheese was kosher? She had never bought anything on her own. Her father was always there to buy it with her. She politely said no and headed for the local market in town.

Masuda listened to the conversations around her. Most people in Aleppo spoke Arabic and French equally. France's soldiers roamed the streets, while its officials ruled the country. Syrians waited anxiously for the French to move out of Syria just as the British had moved out of Iraq. Only the Jews appreciated the ever-present protection of the French.

A French officer reached into his pocket and handed a coin to a woman on a corner selling goat's milk. Masuda stared at the officer, wishing she could count on his protection, or at least on his help to find her uncle. But she had to be very careful. It was hard to tell exactly who was involved in the plan to assassinate her father and exactly how far this plan reached. All the way to Aleppo? Possibly.

Masuda crossed the street. "Excuse me, sir," she said, deepening her voice. "I am looking for the Jewish Quarter."

"If it's the Old City you want, you have a long walk ahead, but it's hard to get lost. Keep on this road over here and once you get to the *souk*, just ask. The Old City is quite cramped. You'll find the Jews there soon enough."

It was not until hours later that she finally reached the Old City of Aleppo. Along the way, she stopped at the *habbaz*[1] for bread, at the well to fill up the water pouch and at any vendor who was kind enough to offer shade from the afternoon sun.

---

1. **habbaz** – (Arabic) baker.

She looked around, half worried and half enjoying the new sounds and flavors of Syria. The rocky city of Aleppo was busy but quieter than Iraq. On the roads, women sat outside their homes, squatting on the ground and preparing their dinner. The sun had been falling for a couple of hours now. Masuda was sure that sunset would not wait for her. Was she ever going to find her uncle?

Humming from Aleppo's eight kilometer *souk* spilled out onto the streets. Masuda wiggled her foot to relieve her heel from the leather strap that cut into her skin. She sat back on a stone stump at the side of the road near a vegetable stall, relieving her legs for a moment. She unraveled the strap around her ankle and examined her bleeding foot. If she had a knife, she could cut off the back straps altogether, she thought.

Without warning, an old man shoved her off the stump. Masuda fell over, pressing her hands ahead to catch her fall.

"Who do you think you are? This has been my seat for thirty years!" the old Arab screeched, towering over her.

Masuda scampered away, trying to focus her eyes, which vibrated inside their sockets.

"*Shihwaar il neel!* Black Nile muck!" he muttered after her.

Without much caution, she rubbed the dirt off Jamil's robe, breathlessly staggering into the nearest opening of the *souk*.

Masuda looked up at the walls and roofs made of stone that shaded the thirteenth century marketplace. Each street of the organized chaos represented a different craft. The silversmiths, the jewelers, the leather tanners, the carpet makers, the spice traders, each claimed a different street with their sharp odors and loud chatter.

Inside the *souk*, she asked the same question but the responses varied. The lady dusting off a row of silver pleading to be polished waved her off. The man pulling down carpets from the walls of his stall motioned to the jewelry market. When she found a jeweler who finally looked up from his eyepiece, he said, "When you leave the *souk*, take that road," he pointed with his right hand, "take it up past Antaki. Keep walking until you pass the Akabe Quarter. Walk a little more and you will find the Jewish Quarter of Bahsita. There are not many Jews living there but their Knees-il-Kibbireh still stands tall."

"Knees-il-Kibbireh," repeated Masuda before thanking the jeweler. That's it!

She plunged into the street and tilted her head upward. "Thank you, Hashem."

CHAPTER TEN

*K*NEES-IL-KIBBIREH STOOD IN THE JEWISH QUARTER OF Bahsita in the Old City of Aleppo. Masuda's mother had always referred to it as the Great Synagogue of Aleppo. She remembered the name well as it was attached to many of her favorite bedtime stories. Several quarters made up the Old City, mazed with their narrow winding streets. And although most Jews had moved out of the Jewish Quarter to live in more comfortable neighborhoods outside the Old City, they continued to support the synagogues and Jewish institutions that still remained there.

As the sun tucked itself behind any traces of day, shades of orange and dark blue trimmed the horizon. The soles of her feet were hot and covered with dust. Blisters formed between the bleeding cuts where the sandal's straps wrapped her ankle. A dull sensation in her body reminded her of the unpleasant encounter with the old Arab outside the *souk*. But her pain disappeared as the walls of the Great Synagogue came into view. She stared at the sight and could see the symbol of strength it represented throughout time for the Jews of Aleppo. She held onto a wall of the outer courtyard, remembering tales of Jews hiding within these walls for protection from riots, wars and even blood libels.

Masuda slowly entered the outer courtyard of the synagogue, looking up at its massive three-story structure.

Rows of arches framed the entrance. With awe in her eyes, she took a deep breath before stepping into the main sanctuary.

Inside, white walls and dark wooden benches filled the room. Mr. Attie, the *shamosh*,[1] stood by the *bimah*[2] with a pile of prayer books in hand. He turned at the sound of Masuda's footsteps. Mr. Attie stepped back and set down the pile of books on a red tapestry that stretched evenly over the *bimah*. "Yes? Can I help you?"

Masuda looked around at the familiar surroundings — the *siddurim*[3] stacked high against one wall, a stone *bimah* surrounded by wooden benches and the *ner tamid*,[4] its light glowing on the gold stars embroidered into a red velvet curtain covering the *heichal*.[5] They all seemed to lie across her shoulders, filling her heart with comfort, while at the same time lodging a big lump in her throat.

"Who are you?" the *shamosh* asked.

"I'm sorry," Masuda wiped her eyes, stopping her tears. "I am a Jewish girl traveling to Syria in search of my uncle." She looked up at the *agal* sliding over her forehead. Slowly, she removed it along with the long scarf hanging down over her shoulders. Her big brown eyes looked even bigger framed by her tight dark curls.

Mr. Attie leaned against the bench at his side, easing himself into a seat, his eyes staring at the *agal* in Masuda's hand.

"Who is your uncle?"

"Robert Matalon," she said, her voice quivering.

"Matalon, yes. I do know a Matalon…from Baghdad?" he asked, looking over her baggy robe.

---

1. **shamosh** – (Hebrew) caretaker of a synagogue.
2. **bimah** – (Hebrew) a platform, usually raised, where the *Sefer Torah* is read.
3. **siddurim** – (Hebrew) prayer books.
4. **ner tamid** – (Hebrew) eternal light.
5. **heichal** – (Hebrew) the main ark where the Sifrei Torah are kept.

Masuda's face lit up at the recognition of her uncle. Here was someone who understands, who knows her family, who can help her to safety.

"If your uncle is the same good soul I am thinking of, I know him very well indeed. In fact, he takes care of a lot of the synagogue's business. You can't even get a look at the sacred *Keter Torah*[1] or any of the ancient scrolls without him." Mr. Attie reached into his pocket and handed a white handkerchief to Masuda.

"Thank you," she said, remembering the dirt she had smeared on her face while she was on the train.

"Your uncle lives in Djamiliyeh. I can try to locate him and get word to him that you are here. Where are you…staying?" he asked.

Masuda shook her head. "I will be staying with my uncle. That is why I need to find him."

"I see," Mr. Attie said, scratching his short beard. "There *is* one small problem. Djamiliyeh is a good hour and a half walk from here and the trolley has not been running well today. If that is still the case, you will have to find some-place else to stay until we can get word to your uncle."

Masuda spoke in a low voice. "There is no other place."

"You are welcome to come to my brother's house. It's not far from here," Mr. Attie offered. "That is where I live."

Masuda shook her head at the thought. "I need to see my uncle. He will take care of everything."

"I understand that," said the *shamosh* patiently, "but all that might have to wait until daylight."

Mr. Attie looked at Masuda for a response to his invita-tion. Confusion swayed in her eyes, and her face grew hot. How could she go home with this strange man? It is true that in the last twelve hours, she had gone against certain

---

1. **Keter Torah** – (Hebrew) "Crown of the Torah"; also known as the Aleppo Codex. A Bible text on parchment kept in book form, with vowels and accents. The text was written and pointed by Aharon ben Moshe ben Asher in the 9th century, C.E. It is the oldest known reference for writing a *Sefer Torah* today.

truths and done some questionable things, but she knew very well that this was different, even after all that.

The *shamosh* spoke up. "I have a good idea. I know a place where you will be very comfortable. You will be able to enjoy the company of girls your own age and I can walk you there myself. I will take you straight to my aunt Latifeh."

"And when will I be able to see my uncle?" she asked.

"As soon as I can contact him. If I have to, I will take you there myself," Mr. Attie answered.

Not her first choice, but Masuda agreed.

CHAPTER ELEVEN

"**R**IGHT NOW!" A VOICE ECHOED DOWN THE HALL.
Masuda shuddered beside the *shamosh* in the entranceway of the orphanage. Only now did she learn that Aunt Latifeh was the headmistress at the orphanage and that this was to be the safe, comfortable place where she would fit in and enjoy her stay the most.

The smells of bland soup and boiling soap hung in the air. Masuda looked around at the old, peeling walls that seemed to stare back at her, telling her that she didn't belong. The *shamosh* stepped forward. "Morah Latifah?" he called softly.

"Yes. Who's there?"

Masuda smoothed her hair and lowered her eyes down her dress, stopping short at the sight of Jamil's sandals — ragged, oversized and out of place. She felt slightly relieved that she had taken a few minutes at the synagogue to wash up and remove Jamil's robe and *kaffiyeh*.

Morah Latifah strode down the hall as if she had done so for a long time. Her hand swung as straight as a stick beside her with each quick stride she took. She had a walk that spelled out authority, and Masuda knew instantly that she was in charge.

"Who is calling for me?" she asked as she turned the corner.

"It's me," the *shamosh* answered.

Morah Latifah slowed her pace as she noticed Masuda

standing beside her nephew. "Some respect, that nephew of mine, calling me his Morah! How old do you think I am?"

The *shamosh* chuckled at her annoyance.

Morah Latifeh's apron reached all the way to her ankles, just above her small black shoes, and the white scarf she wore around her head was so tight, it appeared to Masuda that it was the scarf which was wearing her head and not the other way around. She looked questioningly at Masuda, "And you, young lady?"

"I ..." Masuda started to say. Did everyone have to know her life story? She looked to the *shamosh*. Couldn't he speak for her? This way she wouldn't be forced to say anything that she would rather keep to herself. She avoided Morah Latifeh's stare. If she kept quiet long enough, the *shamosh* would probably jump in; most adults did.

"She came into the synagogue, trying to locate her uncle," he finally said, waving his hand quickly, "but there is no time for that now. He lives somewhere in Halab. It was getting dark and I figured —"

"Don't say another word. She is welcome to stay here as long as it takes to find her uncle. Now if you'll come with me, young lady." She motioned to Masuda. "We too must finish our nighttime preparations. It will be a wonder if everything gets done."

Masuda turned to the *shamosh*, who said, "You are in good hands. Morah Latifeh, my aunt, is the headmaster here. I will try to locate your uncle as soon as I can. I know where to find you. Good night and good year." And with that, he was off.

Masuda followed Morah Latifeh through the kitchen. Her stomach growled at the sight of fresh bread stacked in the corner. Steam rose from a pot set on a kerosene stove along the wall.

"You are lucky you arrived today. We received a delivery of fresh bread this morning," Morah Latifeh told her.

Masuda tried to smile.

Morah Latifeh lifted her head and shouted, "Morah Esther! Morah Esther!" she repeated without waiting for a response.

Beyond the kitchen sat two classrooms lined with desks. Morah Latifeh peeked into each one. "Oh, where did she go now? Morah Esther!" She looked back at Masuda. "You will find everything you need here. At the orphanage, we bathe only once a week, on Friday. Today is Wednesday, but I guess we can make an exception. By the looks of you," she said, measuring Masuda with her eyes, "I can tell that you are not too fat, which means that you should probably fit into one of the spare uniforms. Morah Esther! Where is that woman?"

A slender woman hurried down the hall. "Yes, you were calling me?"

"Finally!" Morah Latifeh let out a sigh. "This young lady needs our assistance. We are not yet certain for how long. She asked my nephew to help her locate her uncle here in Halab. For now, she will stay with us. Let's help her get washed up. Good?"

"That will be fine," Morah Esther agreed.

Morah Latifeh whipped off her apron and tossed it into the kitchen.

Morah Esther bent her slender figure and gently placed her hand on Masuda's shoulder. "What is your name, child?"

This was the first time anyone asked her that since she had left her father. It had been easier that way too, no one knowing who she was and where she came from. That way, she was able to move about as she pleased, without anyone caring or getting in the way. But with this woman it seemed different. She didn't look down at her with the look of pity that Masuda was expecting. She smiled gently, the way she knew her mother would if she were still alive today. Morah Esther's smile reached a part of Masuda's heart that was empty and yearning for love. This was a part of her which her father had tried to fill each day. But it was different with this stranger, different because Masuda sensed that she understood, that she could almost see right through her. "Masuda," she answered finally, "Masuda Matalon."

CHAPTER TWELVE

*M*ASUDA BATHED IN A HUGE HAMMERED POT THE SIZE OF a small bathtub with a wooden stool in the center. She sat on the stool while Morah Esther poured the almost warm water over her head. Masuda rolled the rough ball of soap between her hands, praying that no one else would walk in.

"Here is a clean uniform," Morah Esther said, holding the white dress up for Masuda to see. Then she handed Masuda a dry towel. "Maybe you would like to wear it while you let this dress of yours dry." She pulled Masuda's dress out of a small basin of soapy water and rinsed it in clear water before wringing it out.

Morah Esther snapped the dress in the air, shaking out the excess water. Masuda wrapped a towel around her body and stared at her flat dress flapping in the air. It was all she had left. She was now without her father, without the things that her mother left for her, without anything else from her home and her thirteen years of living except for this old white dress! Of course she still had her book, she thought.

Masuda glanced over to where Morah Esther smoothed out her wet dress. "Wait, my *Tanach*!"

Morah Esther looked up from the washbasin and turned around.

"I'm sorry," Masuda said, "I meant … in my pocket … inside the dress I left a —"

"This?" Morah Esther said, holding up Masuda's *Tanach*, the one her father had given her. "I removed it before washing the dress. And this?" she held up Masuda's money in her other hand. "I have a small pouch perfect for holding your valuables. It's yours if you want it."

"Thank you," said Masuda. She smiled at the one shred of hope that would get her through this. Not the money, of course, and not Morah Esther's pouch either, although she did appreciate her kindness. It was the *Torah* that warmed her heart. She quickly dressed and fingered her book as she followed Morah Esther down the hall. She turned to the page with her father's inscription. There it was. *G-d has blessed you. Keep his words with you always.* It was all her father ever asked of her. She closed the *Tanach* and held it close. She would read some *Tehillim*[1] while she was here, as soon as she had the chance. And from the looks of things, it didn't seem to Masuda that finding the time would be a problem. The inside of the orphanage looked as plain and as uninteresting as the flat bread her father bought on the streets of Baghdad — pale and empty with dusty surfaces all over.

Screeching and yelping came from the girls' sleeping quarters. Morah Esther knocked softly on the door before entering. Immediately, the noise halted and everyone stood up straight. But as they sighed with relief, Masuda suspected that it was not Morah Esther who they feared it would be.

They all stared equally at Masuda as if waiting for her to reveal her entire life to them.

A small girl in the corner broke the silence, "We all thought you were Morah La —"

The taller girl standing beside the smaller one shoved her elbow into the girl's arm and glared at her with her lips pinched.

Tehillim – (Hebrew) psalms

Morah Esther turned to the taller girl. "Sylvia," she said in a sweet but stern voice, "I am sure that you and all your friends will be happy to know that Hashem has blessed us with a lovely guest tonight. This," she turned around, "is Masuda. I am counting on you all to set up her bedding and make sure she has all she needs here while I see to a different matter."

"As long as I don't have to share my bed like I did the last time, when —," Sylvia interrupted.

A chorus of giggling burst into the room.

"Sylvia, you sound so concerned. In that case, you can be the first to help." Morah Esther pointed to the wall. "The mattress please. Rivka, you can get the bedding." She turned to the small girl who was still wincing and holding her bruised arm. "Tunie, you can rest your arm now. I am sure that Sylvia will get you anything you need as soon as she sets up the mattress."

The rest of the little girls cried out in unison, "Me too, I want to help!"

"That is good. Everyone can help and I will see all of you later."

Masuda turned to Sylvia, who was already heaving the mattress off the pile against the wall.

"Can I help?" Masuda asked.

Sylvia looked up at Masuda. "Sure, big eyes. Grab the other end."

Masuda pulled on the mattress, dragging it to an open space on the floor.

"You are lucky that you came in today. Penina left a couple of days ago. This was her mattress. She was adopted by a family who said they would love her and give her an—y—thing she needs," she said in a high-pitched voice.

"Don't believe her," said Rivka, hiding behind the linens piled in her arms.

"Oh, and she should believe you? Our long legged, dark

skinned friend from Yemen?" Sylvia snapped.

Rivka threw the pile of linens down on the mattress and planted her arms on her hips. Sylvia lifted her fists with a mocking gesture.

Masuda stepped back in shock, almost sorry she had offered to help in the first place.

Tunie slid beside Masuda and whispered, "Don't be so scared. They're just playing around."

Rivka eyed her friend a little longer and then bent down on her knees. She spread open a sheet and stretched it over the mattress that lay on the floor.

"Thank you," Masuda said, as she took a gray blanket from the pile and stretched it on top of the sheet.

No one responded.

Was she expected to live with these people? She was not an orphan! Well, not a full orphan anyway. Her mother had passed away, but she had a father and he would come for her as soon as he could. Masuda folded one side of the sheet over the top of the blanket and tucked it under the mattress. As she smoothed the wrinkles in the blanket with her hand, she thought, what if her father did not return? That would make her a full orphan and this place would be her home. She drew in a deep breath. Soon she would be at her uncle's, she said to herself as she kissed her book and slipped it under the pillow.

CHAPTER THIRTEEN

AFTER DINNER, MORAH LATIFEH TOLD A STORY, JUST AS she had been doing every night since she began working at the orphanage. She ended with, "The Jewish girl is like a diamond wrapped in brown paper. The outside doesn't matter. In the end, it gets crumpled up and discarded. It is the treasure inside which counts. This is the Jewish girl — hidden, brilliant and priceless."

Later, Masuda thought about what Morah Latifeh had said. She lay awake, staring at the ceiling, enjoying the idea of being brilliant and priceless, but hoping there would never come a day when she would be crumpled up and discarded.

She shifted her heavy legs and winced as the sheet caught one of the blisters on her foot. But no matter where she moved, she could not escape the hard and lumpy spots in the mattress. She missed her bed at home. It sat in a painted frame covered by a soft cotton blanket and every once in a while someone would come with brass rods to shake up all the stuffing in her mattress until it was light and fluffy again.

Silence crept into the room as Masuda pulled the itchy blanket over her arms. Her tossing and turning left her on her back, looking up at the cracks in the ceiling. There were so many — some were rounded, shaped like fat bananas, and others were sharp and long, like lightening bolts. She wondered how long they had been there. But the more she stared, the more the ceiling seemed to drop lower and lower, splitting and splintering, until she could no longer look.

Tunie sat up in bed, breaking the silence. "What kind of a name is Masuda?"

Masuda lifted her head. Just a little bit longer with these girls and I'll be gone, she reminded herself. She snuggled back under her covers, hoping they would leave her alone so that she could get some sleep.

Tunie tried again. "What does it mean? Sylvia said that Masuda is the fat under a camel's hump. But I don't believe her."

"I did not!" Sylvia screamed out. "And besides, how would you know? You've never really been outside the walls of this orphanage. Have you ever sat on a camel?"

"Stop bullying her!" Rivka called out from the other side of Masuda.

Masuda was hoping to say as little as possible until she arrived at her uncle's house. She had gotten this far by herself, without opening up to anyone, without getting hurt.

Masuda could hear Tunie whimpering. She wailed into her pillow for more then a few minutes and long after the other girls had fallen asleep.

Masuda stretched her arm over the foot of her bed and tapped Tunie on the arm. Not that she needed to explain the real meaning of her name for the bully's sake, but for Tunie. Masuda would leave soon, but Tunie would stay here. She could at least answer her question.

Tunie looked up, trying to catch her breath.

"Masuda means luck," she said.

"Really?" Tunie asked, her voice hoarse.

"Really. And you are smart to ask." And then for no reason at all, she added, "Imagine if Masuda really did mean the fat under a camel's hump."

And they both laughed.

CHAPTER FOURTEEN

*L*IGHT PEERED THROUGH THE SMALL WINDOW. THE SUN WOKE Masuda, warming her face and inviting her to greet the day. She tried to get up, to even roll over, but her legs felt as heavy as iron and her back ached, all the way up to her neck.

She opened her eyes. Most of the mattresses were empty and already made. Rivka walked into the room, heading straight for Masuda. "You're still in bed?"

Masuda sat up, squinting from the light.

"Morah Esther said that you weren't to be disturbed this morning and that you would join us when you were good and ready. But Morah Latifeh just sent me to let you know where we would be."

"Thank you," Masuda said, slipping into her uniform. She reached for the sandals Morah Esther had given her; used, but in good condition.

"I would shake those out if I were you," Rivka said, pointing to the sandals. Then she lowered her voice and curved her hand at the side of her mouth. "Centipedes," she whispered.

They walked together down the dark halls to the other side of the orphanage. "We just started prayers, but don't worry, you can catch up."

Just a little while longer, Masuda reminded herself. Her stomach rumbled. Her tongue stuck to the roof of her mouth. "Where can I get some water?"

"There is a pitcher in the kitchen. I'll show you the way."

After prayers and some hours of study in the classroom, everyone sat down to lunch in the courtyard.

Three tables stood alongside the high walls of the outdoor courtyard, the overhead sun casting shadows on their splintered legs. A flat piece of bread and a bowl of hot *fassoulyeh*[1] marked each place setting.

With her spoon, Masuda stirred the bean stew, searching for but not expecting a soft piece of meat, which normally buried itself between the beans. But a bone with a string of meat attached was all she found.

The doors to the courtyard swung open. Señor Dwek walked in with a white suit and a white hat. Morah Latifeh hurried over to greet him and escorted him to the table. The overseer of the orphanage reached into his pocket and handed out candy to the children.

On the bench, Sylvia leaned in closer to Masuda. "Señor Dwek comes all the time to check up on us. Sometimes he comes with Rabbi Laniado, who tests us on our studies. Tunie thinks that Señor Dwek is her father."

"No she doesn't," Masuda said.

Tunie ran up to hug the man. He opened his hand to her. Three pink sugar coated almonds rolled in his palm. "Thank you!" Tunie said, scraping them up.

"He is the only man she ever knew. We all go along with her. She came into the orphanage as an infant. No one knows why. At least, that's what they tell us," explained Sylvia.

"And you?" Masuda asked, only because she sensed that Sylvia wanted her to.

"Do you want to hear the real story, or the one Morah Latifeh told me when I was old enough to understand?" Sylvia pushed to get out of her seat, and threw her legs over the bench.

---

1. **fassoulyeh** – (Arabic) bean stew.

Masuda wasn't sure if she wanted her to follow or if she just wanted to get away from everyone. It was hard to tell with Sylvia. Masuda slipped out of the bench and followed Sylvia past the trees that outlined the courtyard.

As Masuda caught up, Sylvia spoke, looking straight ahead. "I first came to the orphanage when I was five years old. The first five years that I lived in the orphanage, I never asked about my parents. I just accepted the fact that my parents 'passed away' exactly like they told me. When I was ten, I had to know why, or how, or something."

Masuda tucked a loose curl behind her ear.

"Morah Latifeh told me that my mother and father both passed away tragically in a train accident just before I was brought here. Even when I stopped crying, I could think of nothing else. I asked if there were some pictures or something, anything about my family. But she said no. She told me that the orphanage was my family now and I should try to forget about my parents, the sooner, the better."

Masuda stared blankly at Sylvia, waiting for her to go on.

"I even went through Morah Latifeh's papers to find some proof to what she had told me. That is when I found out the *real story*."

"What did you find out?"

Sylvia clasped her hands together. "Morah Latifeh hides a big trunk down in the cellar. There she keeps everything ever known about the orphans here." Sylvia looked over her shoulder. "I found a letter from my mother to Morah Latifeh. It was my father who died in a train accident. My mother wrote the letter to explain why she was placing me in the orphanage and why she could no longer take care of me herself. That was the real story."

Masuda's heart sank. She often thought about her own mother. Her father was always there to fill in the parts of her life that she couldn't remember, especially those involving her mother.

Sylvia was different. She stood, holding in her tears and rubbing her finger down the bumpy stone wall of the courtyard. She had no mother or father. Her mother had given her up. She had not wanted to raise Sylvia anymore and Sylvia knew it.

"Did you tell Morah Latifeh that you found out?"

"No, I never did. But I think that Morah Esther knew. She sat on my mattress every night for a whole week and rubbed my back and sang me to sleep." Sylvia spun around and grabbed Masuda's hand. Her watery eyes looked sadly at Masuda. "I have never said a word to anyone about this."

Masuda took Sylvia's hands in hers. "Then I have no reason to say anything either."

"Don't look now, but here she comes," Sylvia said.

Masuda turned around. Morah Latifeh waved toward Masuda with her handkerchief, clearing her path.

Masuda backed against the wall, hoping she hadn't done anything wrong. "Masuda!" Morah Latifeh was shouting. "Masuuuda!" she repeated her name, louder this time, like a birdcall.

Masuda stepped forward.

"What are you waiting for, child? I haven't all day!" She came to an abrupt halt.

"Let's go," she said, pulling Masuda by the hand. "Señor Dwek is waiting. He wants to speak to you."

Señor Dwek stepped forward, tilting his white-brimmed hat. "Miss Matalon, it is a pleasure to meet you," he said. "Mr. Attie, the *shamosh*, told me about your situation. I happen to know your uncle."

"You do?" Masuda tried not to sound too excited. "Did you speak to him?"

"I have tried. However, no one answers at his home. A neighbor tells me that the entire family is expected back tonight or tomorrow. I will try to get in touch with him then.

You know with *kapparot*[1] tonight, it may be difficult."

"I'm sure my aunt and cousins will certainly be home, even with *kapparot*."

"We will just have to see about that. Be patient. By tomorrow, this time, you will be with your family at last." He looked at Morah Latifeh who stood nearby, listening. "Did you have a pleasant stay here?"

"Yes," Masuda said. "I am very grateful. Everyone has been most kind."

Morah Latifeh announced that everyone was required to rest in preparation for *kapparot* that night. Taking a nap after the afternoon meal was never easy for Masuda, and it seemed that this custom did not stop with her family or even with the Jews of Baghdad. Practically everyone had this custom, but that was only on Shabbat.

Masuda knelt on her mattress and reached under the pillow for her *Tanach*. She walked over to a small window in the sleeping quarters. There, she opened her book, reading through the holy words and phrases of Perashat Yom Kippur.[2] Suddenly, she stopped reading and her eyes sat heavily on the second chapter from the book of Yonah. She read:

Waters encompassed me to the soul, the deep whirled around me;
Reeds were tangled about my head
I descended to the bases of the mountains;
The earth — its bars (were closed) against me forever.
Yet, You lifted my life from the pit, O Hashem, my G-d.

---

1. **kapparot** – (Hebrew) the practice of offering the life of a fowl as a scapegoat, to atone for the sins of an individual. This Jewish ritual is done prior to Yom Kippur.
2. **Prashat Yom Kippur** – (Hebrew) the Torah reading designated for the holiday of Yom Kippur.

A single tear rolled down her face as she thought of what had become of her life since Monday afternoon. She stared at the last verse and hoped that her ending would be at least as good as Yonah's.

Naptime quickly came to an end. For the next hour Masuda played jacks, popping the ball into the air and scooping up the little wood squares. Tomorrow at this time she would be in her uncle's house, she told herself. But for the moment, she laughed, beating anyone who came to challenge her, except for Tunie. When Tunie joined in, she let her win on purpose. And it was worth it to see her face gleaming in victory.

"Are you going to stay?" asked Tunie. "Because I like you, Masuda!"

Chapter Fifteen

*I*T DIDN'T SURPRISE MASUDA THAT HE WAS ABOUT TO slaughter the chickens right in the middle of the courtyard. She had seen the Jewish tradition of *kapparot* done before. At home, in Baghdad, the stone slabs of her courtyard were still stained with streaks of red and purple because no one had thought to cover the ground first. But at least at home they kept the slaughtering to one side, near the corner date tree.

Inside the orphanage, Masuda wrapped the gray scratchy blanket around her shoulders. She dusted off the bottom of her dress and ran her hands over her raven curls. They sprang back as if they had never been disturbed. The soap she now used to wash her hair left it looking and feeling like braided yarn that had been wetted, dried and then unraveled. At home, she had a special soap, just for hair. Her father bought her the gentlest soaps, made from the richest oils. Her father. She didn't want to worry about him now. Not even to think about him. She missed him too much. Her heart sank further with each day that passed. She yearned to speak with him, for him to scoop her up in his arms and take her back home. But how could he come for her now? He didn't even know where she was.

And it wasn't like anyone would find out either. Aside from Señor Dwek, no one came to visit the orphanage. It was much different in Baghdad, where the days were filled with visitors, laughter and singing. She especially enjoyed Shabbat, when every stroll usually ended up at the rabbi's house for inspiration and guidance.

There were no visitors here. Not even the strange neighbors of the orphanage, who dumped their trash out their windows, came to visit. And it seemed that no one, absolutely no one, left the orphanage — except for the teachers, Morah Latifeh and Morah Esther, when it suited them.

Masuda took in a deep breath, thinking about tomorrow, when her uncle would come for her. Maybe tonight. But she didn't want to get her hopes up. Tomorrow would be fine. This way, she wouldn't have to miss the traditional *kapparot* about to take place.

Screams of laughter came from the courtyard. It had started. Masuda lifted her skirts and leaped across the floor. When she had been little she had pressed her eyes shut with her fingertips at the thought of it. But now, especially without her father, *kapparot* was a time-honored tradition she did not want to miss.

Outside, Masuda skipped across the courtyard. The stench of chicken urine and droppings enveloped her all at once. Her new friends, Sylvia, Tunie and Rivka, sat against the towering fountain embedded in the center of the courtyard. The nine-day-old moon glowed under a tent of dancing stars, casting its light on her friends. Their shadows extended to almost four times the length of their hunched-over bodies. But Morah Esther's shadow was the longest as she stood up against the sky. The presence of Masuda's new caretaker comforted her, especially when Morah Latifah was around.

Masuda stepped in closer, her eyes trapped on the wooden crate of bouncing white feathers and bobbing beaks. The chickens cackled and balked, writhing for territory inside the eucalyptus walls of the bird crate. She slid to the ground, tucking her cape under her legs, above the stone floor that left no traces of warmth from the day's sun.

Next to the pen of screeching birds, a man with a white apron, whom she assumed was the *shohet*,[1] picked up a long knife and slowly slid his fingernail up and down its sharpened edge. Up and down. Up and down. Then, he put down the knife he was inspecting and stretched his arm into the big wooden box. When he pulled it out, his hand was tightly clenched around the closed wings of the first female chicken.

Morah Latifeh strode over. She looked up at the *shohet* and planted her black leather shoes firmly on the ground. "I am first!"

The *shohet* looked around as if waiting for someone to contest her bold remark. Then she whispered something to the *shohet* and lowered her head in prayer. The *shohet* held the dangling hen in his right hand and circled it around Morah Latifeh's head as he recited the blessing for her over and over, "This is your atonement, this is your exchange, this is your barter. This is your atonement, this is your exchange, this is your barter." A lock of her hair swayed in the night air, escaping the cotton handkerchief knotted at the back of her neck.

Masuda rose up on her knees, listening to the even chanting of the bearded man. She closed her dark eyes and breathed in the familiar words that kissed her soul and opened the gates of Yom Kippur.

She liked the idea that all of her sins were being transferred to the chicken. After turning twelve and accepting upon herself all the commandments of the Torah, she supposed that she needed all the help she could get.

Rivka shifted beside Masuda. "Did you do *kapparot* this way in Baghdad?" Rivka asked.

---

shohet – ritual slaughterer

Masuda turned to her as if awakened from a dream. "Yes," she stammered, her thoughts still locked on the ritual. "But in Baghdad, they slaughtered the chickens right in front of you. My father always made me look."

"Just wait," answered the dark skinned girl from Yemen. "It has only begun."

Suddenly Sylvia screamed out, losing all sense of caution.

Masuda shifted onto her knees to get a better look. "Is she all right?"

"I think so," answered Rivka, pointing to Sylvia who was now doubled over in laughter.

The frightened chicken swinging over Morah Latifeh's head sprayed a circle of droppings that fell to the ground, sending the girls crawling backward. The laughter was contagious. But the wood ruler sticking out of Morah Latifeh's coat quieted them all down to a soft giggle.

Morah Latifeh let out a shriek after realizing that the yellowy mushy driblets she swiped off her head were coming from the squirming hen. She looked up at the *shohet*. "It is probably a good sign," she said, telling more than asking. He closed his eyes and shrugged his shoulders like he did so many other times that day, "Maybe."

A series of hens were yanked out of the wooden crate as everyone had her turn. Morah Latifeh was followed by Morah Esther, who was followed by Sylvia, Rivka, Tunie and Masuda. The younger orphans were asleep in the apartment at the other end of the courtyard, but six chickens were used in their names as well. One male chicken, the rooster, was reserved at the end for Rabbi Laniado, who walked with a limp and said that he would never miss an event at the orphanage if he could help it.

All the girls covered their eyes as the *shohet* slit the throat of the first chicken in one quick motion. All except for Masuda. She stared at the last signs of life slipping away from the bird, even after Morah Esther gave her a gentle nudge to let her know it was time to go inside. Her eyes wanted to hold onto this tradition that reminded her so much of her father and her life in Baghdad. Her heart jittered with joy and gratitude and sadness and fear. She needed to hold on...to trap that faith and take it with her. To believe that he was safe and that he would follow her as surely as Yom Kippur would follow the next sundown.

CHAPTER SIXTEEN

ASUDA SPOTTED HER UNCLE STANDING IN THE COURT-yard of the orphanage. His felt hat fit as perfectly as his custom-made three-piece suit. Shorter and slimmer than her father, he wore a thin mustache above his mouth, longer than the usually square-shaped kind, which made her giggle.

The heavy door slammed behind her. "Masuda?" He lifted his chin to see her.

She flew down the uneven steps. "Uncle? Uncle Robert!"

"There she is!" He threw his hands up in the air.

"Uncle Robert!"

"Your father will be happy to know that I have found you!"

"You have spoken to Father? Where is he?" She looked over his shoulder.

"He's not here, but he *is* safe and will be coming soon, hopefully in time for Succot."[1]

"Are you sure?"

Uncle Robert leaned in closer. He smelled of shoe polish and the clean scent of soap. "I spoke to him myself, just last night. Everything is going to be fine. I'm sorry I couldn't come for you sooner. We visited Aunt Sarah's mother in the mountains of Beirut to wish her a good year." Uncle Robert pulled out his timepiece. "Yom Kippur starts tonight. We have much to do and little time to do it. Your

---

1. **Succot** – (Hebrew) the Jewish festival of harvest.

aunt is still waiting for me to pick up some more food for tonight's *seuda*."

Morah Latifeh stepped outside while Morah Esther held the door open for the children.

"Yes, you can all say your good-byes to Masuda. Everyone wave," Morah Latifeh called out.

The girls did not wait for her suggestion to say goodbye to their friend and ran to Masuda, knocking Morah Esther off balance. Each one beamed at Masuda's leaving as if she herself had been chosen — chosen to leave the orphanage, to be part of someone's family. And although Mesuda would never trade places with any of them, she could feel deep down that the good wishes coming her way were a part of their dream, which she had just fulfilled.

"Are you coming back?" Tunie asked.

Rivka took her hand. "Maybe soon. Right?" She stroked Masuda's shoulder.

Masuda climbed the stairs quickly to thank Morah Latifeh, who did not move from the door, except to wave. "Good luck," she called.

Only Morah Esther gave her a warm hug and walked her and Uncle Robert to the *hohsh* door. Then Masuda turned suddenly to say her last good-bye and wrap up this scene, to tuck it away somewhere deep in her heart, to visit when she chose to.

In between the smiles and waving arms stood Sylvia, rubbing her eye.

"Just one more minute?" Masuda asked her uncle. "There is someone I almost forgot."

She stepped through the group and hugged Sylvia softly. Sylvia held on just a little longer. "I wanted to say good-bye," she said.

"I know you did. I will miss you."

Sylvia stepped back as her eyes filled with tears. "I will miss you too. And I *am* happy for you."

"I know," Masuda said before waving to everyone again and turning to leave. She was now ready to join her uncle and pick up the pieces of her life again.

Just as they walked into the street, Uncle Robert turned to Masuda, "Is it true that you traveled to Aleppo on your own?"

Masuda nodded hesitantly. "I had to. It wasn't safe with Mrs. Faraj and her family."

"Did they harm you?" he asked awkwardly.

"No," she said.

"How did you get here?"

"By train."

"Who drove you to the station?"

"I did … it … it was the only way to catch the train for Aleppo, to get away from them."

"You drove the car?" Uncle Robert inhaled, trying to hide his smile. After a small pause, he added, "You did the right thing."

"I just hope Mrs. Faraj finds the car there."

"Don't worry about the car. I'll contact Mrs. Faraj myself. As long as you are safe, that is all that matters."

On the way home, they stopped at the pastry maker to buy *batlawa*.[1] The baker's wife made her own string cheese, which saved them a trip to the cheese maker. The baker wrapped up two packages and they left in a hurry. Robert Matalon reached into his pocket and fished for his timepiece. "Not much time, but we have to make just one more stop." He looked both ways before crossing the street, leading Masuda ahead of him. "There is a very special guest staying with us for the holiday. He is waiting at the Great Synagogue for me — just a quick stop. After that, we really must be getting home."

Masuda turned around, judging how far they had come. "The Great Synagogue is not too far," she said, "just a short walk."

---

1. **batlawa** – (Arabic) Syrian pastry.

"You are starting to feel at home in Aleppo, huh?" her uncle teased her.

Uncle Robert led her through the narrow street to where the synagogue stood. She had been there only a few days ago and yet the grand structure still caught her breath.

"There is a secret about this synagogue," Uncle Robert said, passing through the outdoor courtyard. "It is the home of the legendary *Keter*, actually, it is the *Keter* of Aharon ben Moshe ben Asher."

"It is very old, right?"

"I would say so. It was written by Ben Asher about 1,000 years ago."

Masuda chuckled. "That is old."

"Yes, and quite famous too. People come from all over to see it, it being the oldest source and reference for writing a *Sefer Torah,* even up until today. Rabbi Shtern came all the way from Poland to see it. I met him this morning and have invited him to be our guest for the holidays. After minhah, he insisted on spending the day at the synagogue to prepare his soul...a very righteous man. I agreed to show him the *Keter.*" He glanced once again at his timepiece, "I just hope we have the time."

Masuda's fingertips brushed the decorative black iron gate that skirted around the outdoor *bimah.* Covering the *bimah* was a square roof, domed at the top, with its edges cornered off in a black lace pattern.

"Mr. Attie said that no one can look at the *Keter* without you. Is that true?" Masuda asked.

"Yes."

"But why?"

"Because my dear niece, I have the key to the box where the *Keter* is hidden." He winked at her, dangling the small brass key in the air.

CHAPTER SEVENTEEN

*T*HE TALL STONE ARCHES SEEMED TO LEAD THE WAY, first through the courtyard, and then to the entrance of the synagogue, and they continued to stretch high above Masuda's head until she entered the main sanctuary. There he was. Rabbi Avraham Shtern sat on a bench near the indoor *bimah*, humming a steady tune, his wide body shaking back and forth.

As she stepped in closer, Masuda could hear him. He spoke softly in Hebrew, "Yom Kippur. What will happen? Yom Kippur, what will be?" Then he began crying, holding his eyes shut with his fingers as his shoulders bounced up and down from his sobs.

Masuda looked at her uncle, who seemed to be surprised.

The rabbi's sobs quieted and he moaned the words, "All our sins! What will we do? What will be?"

At that moment, Masuda realized where she had seen the rabbi before. He was the rabbi from the train, the one sleeping in the front of the car before Masuda had startled him.

Uncle Robert walked toward the rabbi and cleared his throat. "Rabbi Shtern?"

Masuda turned away nervously, wondering if the rabbi recognized her.

The rabbi looked up, acknowledging Uncle Robert with a short nod. He stood, wiping his tears with his handkerchief. Then he tucked it into the pocket of his long black coat, which reached nearly to his ankles.

"Rabbi Shtern, are you ready to go now? The entire family is awaiting our arrival. But I know that you are anxious to take a look at the *Keter* before we set out there."

Rabbi Shtern nodded.

Uncle Robert turned quickly to his niece, "Masuda, come with me, I want to show you something in the Cave of Eliyahu HaNavi." She followed her uncle past the *bimah* toward the *heichal* where the smell of burning oil grew stronger with each step she took. Uncle Robert turned into a doorway to the left of the *heichal*. There sat a small room off the main sanctuary, where the smell was the strongest. The lantern hanging from a hook in the middle of the room gave off enough light for her to see the jug of oil and matchsticks against the wall. In the middle of the small room stood a black metal table filled with glowing wicks that floated in oil. Checkered pattern stone slabs stretched across the floor, from wall to wall, meeting the wood paneling that stopped halfway up the wall, just above Masuda's head. High up, above the wood paneling, was a small wooden door, hinged on one side.

"Women come from all over to light the weeks before Yom Kippur," Uncle Robert said, looking around at the bare walls, as if they were lined with silver. Masuda noticed the empty chair in the corner and wondered if it was set aside for Eliyahu HaNavi himself.

She looked over her shoulder to where Rabbi Shtern blew into a tattered handkerchief.

Uncle Robert continued, "We hope that the saintly rabbis buried in the adjacent Cave of the Just will join us in our prayers. Maybe their merit will bring us the proper repentance that we need."

He leaned over and poured a small amount of oil into a

section of the black table and set a wick inside. Then he handed a matchstick to Masuda. "This ark," he said, reaching to unlock the wooden door above his head, "is where we keep the *Keter*." He pulled out a metal box from the ark in the wall and carried it from the small room toward the *bimah* in the main sanctuary, where Rabbi Shtern stood waiting.

Masuda lit a wick and placed the wooden stick down on the metal table, nodding to her uncle that she would be right along. Then she bowed her head and closed her eyes in prayer. Suddenly, all that had happened to her since she had left her home in Baghdad rushed upon her in an unstoppable current. Tears welled up in her eyes. "Hashem," she said, looking up, "I stand humbly before You." She put her face in her hands. "You have been so generous with me, saving me from Jamil and his family, bringing me safely to Syria and leading me to the right people, who offered me a place to eat and sleep and finally bringing me together with Uncle Robert. I stand with nothing to offer You, and yet I have a request. I know that my mother is with You, and I miss her very much, but I still need my father. He is all I have left. Wherever he is, please protect him. Watch over him constantly and bring him back safely. Please write us down, together with all the Children of Israel, in the book of life for health, happiness, peace and good fortune." Then she wiped her wet face with her fingers and looked up at the walls that framed the ark of Eliyahu, appreciating their rusted cracks and crevices as if they spoke of their age and their wisdom.

In the main sanctuary, three steps up on the *bimah*, Uncle Robert turned over a key in his fingers and shifted the metal box to face him.

Rabbi Shtern swayed back and forth, responding only with the raising of his eyebrow.

"There should be a keyhole…two. That is why there must be two men present at the showing of the *Keter*. Each one brings his own key, all the more protection for the holy sefer.[1] That reminds me…just one minute," Uncle Robert said, snapping his fingers, "I must ask the *shamosh* if Eliyahu Abadi was kind enough to leave him the key I asked for this morning."

Masuda walked into the main sanctuary just as Uncle Robert moved toward the hall, constantly looking back, his eye on the *Keter*.

Masuda heard the voice of the *shamosh*, Mr. Attie, approaching. Rabbi Shtern looked away as if she were not there. His beady eyes darted under bushy gray eyebrows.

"Here we are," her uncle said, pointing toward the *bimah*.

Mr. Attie looked up to see Masuda. "You found your uncle. I am happy to see that. Yes?"

Masuda smiled, "Yes."

Mr. Attie and Uncle Robert stepped onto the *bimah* and turned the box around, revealing a lock with two small keyholes. He opened the box. The *Keter* and other manuscripts lay crowded inside.

"Blessed is our G-d," Rabbi Shtern said finally, rubbing his hands together.

Masuda was expecting her uncle to remove one of the old scrolls. Instead, he reached for a big book, with old yellowed parchment.

Rabbi Shtern slipped on his reading glasses.

From where she was standing, the *Keter* looked like one big book, about the size of a woman's hatbox. With great care, they turned the pages, examining the many rows of text that lined the pages.

"Some say Ben Asher had prophecy when he wrote this," said the *shamosh*.

Uncle Robert leaned in closer. "Such a holy work, he had to have."

---

1. **sefer** – (Hebrew) book.

"Yes, indeed," said Rabbi Shtern, "but is this sufficient protection for such a treasure?"

"We do what we can. The rest is up to the Almighty."

"True," added the *shamosh*, "and I have been here long enough to learn that anyone who knows anything about the *Keter* would only wish to protect it. It is written here in the front, that this manuscript is holy to Hashem and should not be sold or exchanged. And of course there is the curse."

"Curse?" Masuda asked in a low voice.

"Yes, there are stories of a well-known curse on anyone who steals, harms or benefits through the *Keter*."

Rabbi Shtern pulled at his beard.

Uncle Robert carefully closed the book and placed it back into the box, sealing the lid tight. "With G-d's help, we will be back."

CHAPTER EIGHTEEN

*W*ITHOUT SAYING A WORD, RABBI SHTERN LOOKED BACK at the synagogue, his eyes tracing its high walls.

Uncle Robert followed his stare. "The Great Synagogue is not even as big as it used to be," he said. "Its original structure was built by King David's general, Yoab ben Serouya, almost three thousand years ago. The walls you see have since been cut down, to keep away the ambitious conquerors, who enjoyed using the massive structure as their trophy."

"In Poland," the rabbi said, looking ahead, "the synagogues are very modest in size. Although the streets of our Jewish Quarters are just as bumpy."

Together they walked through Bahsita, the Jewish Quarter in the Old City of Aleppo. Masuda followed close behind, holding one of the brown paper bags from the pastry maker as they hopped onto the trolley to Djamiliyeh. She sat quietly rocking to the movements and sounds of the trolley as it skated over the new roads. At her uncle's, she would soon see her father — when he was ready to come, when it was safe.

She closed her eyes, trying to form a picture of her father in her mind. Only a patchy image of him appeared, and it wouldn't sit still long enough for her to take a good look. She opened her eyes as the image drifted farther and farther away.

The streets of Syria whisked by them at 32 kilometers per hour. Something about them seemed familiar. Her head spun around as she noticed a corner store with carpets and tapestries draped outside. She recognized the patterns of purple and red and was sure that she had seen them before. Positive of it.

Then it hit her. These were the streets she had walked on foot. Imagine, only two days ago she had walked for hours from Djamiliyeh to the Old City in search of her uncle, only to return and realize that her uncle was in Djamiliyeh the entire time. And although she knew that everything happened for a reason, she wondered what could possibly be the reason for her trip to the Old City and the orphanage?

They stepped off the trolley and walked to the side of the road. With her eyes, Masuda measured Djamiliyeh's main street, certain that the wide, sweeping road was at least six times broader than the narrow streets of the Old City. She walked beside her uncle, hurrying to keep up with him and Rabbi Shtern.

Down the street, she recognized her uncle's house, which she hadn't seen in over two years. Made of light colored stone, it had many windows all covered with painted shutters, except for those in the cellar, which sat bare and dark. No courtyard surrounded the house. It was open to the street. Even the second floor balcony and the wood *succah*[1] in the small backyard were visible from the street. Only a low gate hemmed a small clearing outside their front door. To Masuda, it was as if the street was their courtyard, shared by everyone.

From outside, she could smell the rich aroma of olive oil frying.

---

1. **succah** – (Hebrew) an outside structure used for dwelling on the holiday of Succot.

Rabbi Shern stepped up to the front door and kissed the mezuzah.[1] He removed a handkerchief from his pocket and shook it open before he began to gently dust off the mezuzah. He continued this even after Uncle Robert and Masuda entered the house.

"Sarah?" Uncle Robert called.

Aunt Sarah hurried to greet them. "Robert?" she said, with her usual French accent. "Have you brought Masuda?" Then she stopped short. "Masuda, just look at you. You are practically a lady!" She opened her arms, wrapping them snuggly around her niece. Then she lowered her voice and turned to her husband. "Where is the rabbi?"

Uncle Robert leaned in closer to his wife, "Would you believe, he is dusting off our mezuzah. He is some tsadik,[2] that Rabbi Shtern. You should have seen him this morning with his two pair of tefillin,[3] I saw him myself."

"Hmm." Aunt Sarah smiled at her husband.

Rabbi Shtern stepped in and removed his black hat, while adjusting the kippah[4] on his head.

"Welcome," Aunt Sarah said.

"Mrs. Matalon, I thank you in advance for your hospitality. May the Good Lord bless you and your family, in the book of life, for a promising year." Rabbi Shtern sang the words more than he said them, with a chant that Masuda did not recognize.

"Thank you, Rabbi. Now if you will allow me to show you to your room…right this way…and I can carry that bag for you."

Rabbi Shtern snatched it quickly from the floor as if it were a pot of gold. "You will find that I am very self-suffi-

---

1. **mezuzah** – (Hebrew) a box, fit with a small parchment scroll to hang on a doorpost.
2. **tsadik** – (Hebrew) a righteous man.
3. **tefillin** – (Hebrew) a small leather box containing a parchment scroll. This is worn each morning for prayers.
4. **kippah** – (Hebrew) skullcap.

cient. I don't plan on being a bother."

"No bother at all," Aunt Sarah said, taken aback. She pointed up the stairs, "I will follow you." Then she turned to Masuda, "Masuda, dear, the twins are still sleeping. They are going to be so excited to see you. Your bedroom is up the stairs, to the right, at the end of the hall. A little small, but at least you will have your privacy."

"Thank you."

Aunt Sarah held her skirts in her hand and headed up the stairs. Masuda followed behind. "We'll talk later," she said, before hurrying to catch up with the rabbi.

Masuda passed her hand over the hammered handles that decorated the dark wooden dresser facing her bed. The drawer opened easily when she pulled. It was empty, almost inviting her to fill it. With nothing to put inside, she backed up onto the bed and sat on it. She bounced into the air a few times to feel the soft fluffy cotton beneath her weight. A real bed, just like the one at home. And it felt like home, with the warm colors of the Persian carpet beneath her feet and the white curtains that hung over shuttered windows, letting in just enough light to give the room an appearance of being more spacious. She couldn't help thinking of the orphanage, where its small windows seemed to do the opposite, shrinking the interior of the fortress down to an imaginary size.

Her eyes glided across the brass headboard that framed the bed and the fine cotton bedspread that reached to the floor. Just one thing was missing. Now that she was safe it occupied her thoughts. Her father. At least now, all she had to do was wait. The worst was over and now she could start her life again. Her father would help her do all that, she thought. He would give her the happiness and security she needed. Her uncle said that he was safe and that he was coming. Maybe even in time for Succot, he said. That was just six more days, beating the next Shabbat, in terms of time.

Aunt Sarah stood in the doorway and knocked gently on the door. In her hand was a small bag, "Masuda, can I come in?"

Masuda stood quickly. "Yes, Aunt Sarah."

Aunt Sarah sat on the bed and put her arm around Masuda's shoulder. "Uncle Robert told me what happened, having to travel all by yourself. My poor child."

Masuda looked down, afraid that if she looked into her aunt's eyes, she would break down and cry.

"The dress you left here last year is still hanging in the closet, and I'm sure there are one or two of mine that would fit you perfectly. I realize that you did not bring any of your things with you, so," she handed Masuda the bag she was holding, "here are some things I thought you might be able to use. If there is anything else —"

"My father," Masuda said, as if it were a complete thought. "Uncle Robert said that he would be coming soon. But how...when will he be here?"

"Very soon. You poor thing, you must be so worried. Do not worry, my dear. He is safe."

"How do you know?"

"We know because we received a message from him last night."

"What did he say?"

"He sent a messenger, who first asked about you. Then, the messenger told us just enough to reassure us that your father is far away from any real danger and that he will be coming here as soon as it is possible."

Masuda looked down, avoiding her aunt's stare. "It's just that I...I..."

"It's just that you miss him," Aunt Sarah said. "And he misses you. Soon that will all be history. You will see." She pulled Masuda close to her. Masuda began to cry softly. "You will see."

"I know," Masuda said, not really knowing at all. She wiped

her eyes and took in a deep breath. "When will my cousins be waking up?" she asked, trying to change the subject.

"Hopefully not for a while, or at least not before the rest of us have a chance to prepare for the holiday, including you."

"What do you need help with?"

"You can help by getting yourself ready," Aunt Sarah said, straightening her skirts. She pulled open the closet and dragged out a wide copper pot, which stretched across the foot of the bed. "You can bathe here. I will bring up the hot water. In the meantime, you can get started by filling the pot with enough cold water as soon as the rabbi is done with the bathroom. You never know with men, how dirty they leave things. Trust me, take the pot, you will be more comfortable this way." She turned to leave and then added, "Remember what I said, you will see."

When Masuda stepped into the bathroom, she heard a light jingle skip across the floor. She bent down, tilting her head to see what she had accidentally kicked. Under the sink was a gold ring, standing on its rim. She picked it up and turned it around in her hand. A heavy coin welded on the front showed a small engraving. She held it up to the light. It was an engraving of a woman's face, looking pensively, with the palms of her hands together, her fingertips right under her chin. What a strange engraving, she thought. And yet, at the same time, it looked familiar. Where had she seen it before? She could feel its place in her memory but from where? And from when? She slid it over her finger. It slipped off immediately, as if it were too big for any woman.

But Jewish men did not wear that kind of jewelry, or any jewelry for that matter. She couldn't imagine it belonged to her uncle, and definitely not Rabbi Shtern, with the looks of the holes in his pants that he tried to cover with his overcoat. A ring like that could probably buy him a nice wardrobe.

It must have belonged to one of the housekeepers, she decided at last. But it would have to be a very rich one with very big hands. She laughed to herself as she put the ring down on the edge of the sink to fill up the pitcher of water for her bath.

In her room, she emptied the water into the copper pot and stepped out of her room once again to refill the pitcher. Quickly, she moved out of the way as Rabbi Shtern hurried by and rushed down the stairs, directly across from the bathroom. She had better hurry herself, she thought.

When she fixed the pitcher under the waterspout, she noticed that the ring she had put on the edge of the sink was gone. She had left the room for just a minute. She was certain that she left it there, on the ledge of the sink, where it slightly angled into the bowl. Could it have fallen down the drain? No, the coin was too big to make it through. She moved back, scanning the floor. The only person around was the rabbi, hurrying down the stairs. Then she smiled at herself. That would be ridiculous.

In her room, Aunt Sarah returned with steaming water. As she poured it into the copper pot, which Masuda had already managed to fill halfway, the hot water sizzled and skipped across the surface.

Aunt Sarah rolled up her sleeve before dipping her hand in the pot. "Just right," she said, swirling around the water and shaking her hand over the pot.

"Thank you," said Masuda.

She waited for her aunt to close the door and quickly stepped into the pot. She sank into the warm water thinking about how kind her aunt had been. Or was it pity? No one needed to feel sorry for her. She was doing fine so far, holding her head up until her father arrived. She could handle a lot. Aunt Sarah meant well, she decided. She displayed only kindness, not pity. And after all she had been through, kindness felt just right.

CHAPTER NINETEEN

𝓘N THE KITCHEN, MASUDA CAREFULLY LADLED STEAMING lamb with potatoes into a china bowl. Smelling the thick, hearty stew warmed her insides. Her twin cousins, Sion and Meir, danced between her and her aunt's skirts, playing hide and seek.

"Masuda," her aunt whispered beside her, "Uncle Robert wishes to remind you not to discuss your father with anyone."

Masuda looked up from the bowl.

"Just in case, for your safety as well as your father's," Aunt Sarah added.

Masuda thought about the little piece of advice she had followed all along. But she nodded anyway while wiping off the little bit of stew that trickled down the side of the bowl.

"That's good, Masuda, just hold a towel around it as you bring it inside. It is very hot," said Aunt Sarah.

"Me!" Sion jumped, just missing the platter of fried *kibbe*[1] on the edge of the kitchen counter. Meir reached into a bowl of rice on the kitchen table.

"Hot, Meir!" Aunt Sarah hollered. He pulled back his hand, licking the soft grains that stuck to his palm.

Masuda nudged the door open with her back, entering the dining room, where Uncle Robert and Rabbi Shtern sat. Rich, colorful foods crowded the table. Stuffed eggplant, sliced tomatoes, roasted chicken with rosemary, cracked wheat and

---

1. **kibbe** – (Arabic) a fried torpedo made of cracked wheat and stuffed with meat.

chick peas stained with orange saffron, lamb with potatoes, crisp green beans, okra with tomato sauce and fluffy, white rice were traditional of every holiday, especially Seudat HaMafseket, the last meal before Yom Kippur. Masuda scanned the table, strategically planning how she would fill her stomach enough to fast for the next twenty-five hours.

Aunt Sarah handed Masuda the carving knife. While she carved the chicken, Masuda thought about how long it must have taken Aunt Sarah to prepare it. The koshering alone probably took most of the day. After plucking all the feathers came the process of salting and soaking. Still, even with the housekeeper to clean up, it was a wonder that any of the cooking got done with Sion and Meir around.

"Aunt Sarah?" Masuda asked. "Can I serve Uncle Robert a piece of chicken?"

Aunt Sarah, who was busy filling Rabbi Shtern's plate, turned to her husband.

"Just a small one," Uncle Robert said, passing his plate along.

Masuda looked up, wondering if Rabbi Shtern had recognized her as the Arab on the train. She passed Uncle Robert his plate thinking, maybe he didn't remember their encounter at all.

"I hope you have considered my offer to duplicate the *Keter*," Rabbi Shtern said.

"Surely, Rabbi, you must have treasures of your own in Europe."

"That is true," the rabbi answered, twisting the straggly hairs of his beard. "But nothing of such value has been able to withstand our persecutions. You can't compare our hundreds of years in Europe to your thousands of years here. The *Keter* is simply precious to us all. You will have great merit sharing this priceless antiquity with our brethren in Eastern Europe."

"I thought Europe had copies of it already. Have you checked?" Uncle Robert asked.

"Maybe for a small group of people, unavailable to the masses. Besides, the quality will not compare to the copy I have in mind." Rabbi Shtern leaned in closer, edging his elbows onto the table. "What I want to do is make copies of the *Keter* available to everyone, spreading G-d's glory throughout the world."

Uncle Robert sat silent for a moment, dunking a torn piece of bread into the *tahine*[1] dip. "I will speak to the men at the synagogue. But don't get your hopes up. It is nearly impossible to get anyone from the synagogue to agree to remove the *Keter* from its home, even for a day."

Duplicate the *Keter*, thought Masuda. That might mean weeks, maybe even a month. She would be gone by then with her father, she thought, judging the length of Rabbi Shtern's stay against her father's return, like she did with everything else. Hopefully, her father would return in a couple of days, like Uncle Robert said. Thursday, Erev Succot[2], would be perfect. She would hope for Thursday.

The next day, it was hard for Masuda to think of anything other than her father. Her stomach sat empty and the house fell quiet as the fast of Yom Kippur filled the hours. All work stopped. The only cleaning done was by the housekeeper, and even then, it was only to tidy the house after Sion and Meir caused another one of their disastrous messes.

Masuda tried to bring meaning to the holy day that only came once a year. She closed her eyes and directed her efforts toward begging for forgiveness and yearning for the

---

1. **tahine** – (Arabic) sesame seed paste.
2. **Erev Succot** – (Hebrew) the day preceding the holiday night of Succot.

closeness and comfort that only comes from opening up your heart to Hashem.

For most of the day, Masuda sat in the synagogue, listening to the prayers and chanting that felt so purifying, and it wasn't until Uncle Robert came home and poured himself a cup of water that she realized the fast was over.

CHAPTER TWENTY

*M*ASUDA COULDN'T BE SURE WHAT TIME IT WAS. She knew it was morning, the day after Yom Kippur. Outside her bedroom window, the sun crept overhead. Noontime? She must have been tired. How did she sleep through the twins' morning routine? Her body sat limp, uninterested in doing her mind's bidding until she threw her legs over the side of the bed.

After dressing, she reached into her dresser drawer for the *Tanach* her father had given her and opened the page with the inscription. *Keep His words with you always,* she read. She closed the book and slid it back into the silk covering before dropping it into her pocket. It weighed down in her dress, but she didn't mind. She welcomed its comfort. It was a comfort that told her that she was never alone. More than a book, it was a heritage, which linked her with her people from the beginning of time.

She slowly walked down the stairs, enjoying the quiet that she knew would not last. Then as quickly as she smiled at her thought, the front door opened. In walked Rabbi Shtern, followed by Sion, who jumped through the doorway, wriggling out of his sweater. He looked up at Masuda walking toward him.

"Hello," she said, helping his arm out of the sleeve. "Where is Meir?"

"With Father," he said, pointing outside. "Meir fell!"

"Oh no!" Masuda said.

Sion laughed. "A big boo-boo. Here," he said pointing, "on his knee."

Rabbi Shtern walked past them, heading up the stairs. Sion grabbed a top off the table and began to spin it.

In the kitchen, Aunt Sarah moved around, busily frying *edjeh pataté*.[1] The mixture of grated onions and potatoes mixed with eggs and sprinkled with allspice sizzled in the shape of a flat tomato. Masuda walked up beside her.

"Good morning. I'm glad I didn't wake you. It looks like you needed your sleep." Aunt Sarah said.

Masuda smiled. "Can I slice some tomatoes?" she said, eyeing the red fruit on the counter.

"All right. They should be here any minute."

"They already are."

"Oh, in that case, we can put out the string cheese and olives," Aunt Sarah said, reaching for the ceramic pot with the heavy lid meant to keep the cheese cool for as long as possible.

"Aunt Sarah?"

"Yes?"

"I wanted to ask you: The housekeeper isn't Jewish, right?"

"That's right, she is Muslim. Why do you ask?"

"Because," Masuda said, looking over her shoulder, "I picked up a ring off the bathroom floor. It had a woman's face on it. I thought it might belong to her."

"Well, usually, Muslims don't carve images of people into anything. That would go against their religion. Their decorations are mostly geometric. But you never know."

"I couldn't help but think that I have seen it before."

"The ring?"

"No, the image of the woman. There was something so familiar about it."

---

1. **edjeh pataté**– (Arabic) a fried pancake made from grated potatoes and onions.

"Can I see it?"

"No ... I mean I don't have it. I thought I had it but —"

"Sarah?" Uncle Robert's voice rang through the house, followed by Meir's exploding cry.

Aunt Sarah wiped her greasy hands on her apron. "Yes, I am here!"

Meir squealed and squirmed while Aunt Sarah gently cleaned his scrapes and bruises. The next few minutes were spent trying to console little Meir, who refused to be consoled. Finally Aunt Sarah declared, "Naptime."

Masuda set down the sliced tomatoes on the table in front of her uncle and Rabbi Shtern.

"They went right to sleep, both of them," Aunt Sarah said before peeling off her apron and sinking into the dining room chair.

Uncle Robert lowered his voice. "They have been out from early in the morning. I brought them home right after the meeting in the synagogue. I didn't even have a chance to stop at the *souk*. I'll go after lunch. Maybe then, Rabbi, you can join me and we can discuss the *Keter*. Although the community's leaders refuse to consider letting the *Keter* out of the synagogue, even for a day, they have agreed to let you study it tomorrow for as long as you wish. The *shamosh* and I have offered to be the ones accompanying you while you study the text. They are very protective, you understand."

"I am pleased to hear that."

"So you're not going to copy the *Keter*?" Masuda heard herself ask.

"A man can still hope," Rabbi Shtern answered.

"But it is so ... so old. How will you be able to protect it from possible damage during the printing process?"

"Ahh! A true keeper of the crown!" Rabbi Shtern called out, pointing his fork in Masuda's direction with a wild look in his eyes. "Even our young protect the *Keter*. That is the nature of the Jew. And this is precisely why I want to make it available to all our young."

Masuda shrunk back to avoid his spit spraying across the table, controlling her thoughts to avoid tainting her impression of the rest of the rabbis from Europe.

"Masuda has a point. That is what concerns most of us, not to mention the threat of possible theft. The world-renowned *Keter* has reached scholars outside the Jewish world as well. You cannot imagine the kind of people we have had to deal with."

The rabbi opened his mouth in shock.

"With no reference to you of course, Rabbi," Uncle Robert added quickly. Then Uncle Robert tapped the bread with his hand and kissed his fingertips. "*Sefradaimeh*! The table should always be full!" he said to his wife as he rubbed his stomach.

"Yes, that's right, delicious," agreed Rabbi Shtern.

"*Sahah*. Enjoy it," Aunt Sarah said.

"Sarah, I'm going to take the rabbi for a walk. We'll be back later." Uncle Robert smiled at his niece before opening the door. "Good-bye."

Masuda slipped the mound of string cheese off the plate and wrapped it in its original paper from the store.

"It's a shame the twins were not up to enjoy the meal with us," Aunt Sarah said.

"They will probably wake up hungry and eat even better."

"You are probably right. And getting really smart." Aunt Sarah patted Masuda's arm.

When Aunt Sarah said things like that, Masuda was reminded of her father. He was the only one to encourage her. And even though he did not compliment her often, when he did, she felt that he meant it. Maybe he would walk through that door tomorrow. It was possible.

Instantly, Aunt Sarah ran across the hallway to the front door. She pulled it open and yelled, "Robert! Oh, he's gone. Robert!"

"What is it?" Masuda asked.

"Oh, never mind, I just needed some things for dinner. I guess I can manage to pick them up later…"

"I can catch him. He just left."

"Are you certain, Masuda?" Aunt Sarah asked. "All right then." She seemed to be searching her thoughts, organizing her shopping list in her mind. "More bread, and a vegetable to cook for dinner…and a small piece of chicken for soup. That should do it."

"I'll hurry," said Masuda before leaving.

CHAPTER TWENTY-ONE

*A*S SHE TURNED THE CORNER, SHE COULD SEE A FAINT outline of the men. They were easy to identify, with Rabbi Shtern, marked as a foreigner, in his black coat all the way down to his ankles. She hurried after them until she was almost on top of them. "Uncle Robert?"

Uncle Robert whirled around. "Masuda. What is it?"

"Everything is fine," she said, slowing down. "Aunt Sarah just wanted me to catch you before you left. She needs some things from the store."

"Why don't you join us and we will shop together, good?"

All the markets in Djamiliyeh did not add up to half the *souk* of Baghdad. But the scents and flavors were the same, never failing to stir her memories of home. Besides, it was good to get out.

The squash looked the best, so Masuda filled the bag with the brightest and shiniest green variety. She avoided the oversized kind, which always carried the largest seeds. She held the bag when they left, shading her eyes as soon as she stepped out from under the canopy.

At the butcher, she waited for Uncle Robert to make his selection, more than happy to stand clear of the bloody floors and counters.

"I don't mean to trouble you," Rabbi Shtern started as they left the butcher, "but I am afraid that I am not sufficiently prepared for the nights in Syria. Is there a place where I can buy socks to keep my feet as warm as I like?"

"It will be my pleasure to take you there," Uncle Robert offered. "It is just a small walk outside of Djamiliyeh to the Tillel market. There, the Arabs sell just about everything, whatever it is that you need."

They walked a little off the paved street where it was hot and dusty beneath their feet until they reached the Tillel market. There, vendors sat under cloth-covered canopies, painting the streets with their merchandise — from rich oils and sweet rosewater to vegetables of every color. They walked farther on, past the hanging leather shoes, and entered an opening into a path of draped fabric.

Uncle Robert stopped and turned to Rabbi Shtern. "In here, you should find what you are looking for."

Masuda pushed the cotton fabrics off her face to see a small shop which escaped the sharp noises of the Arab marketplace.

"Welcome! How are you?" the vendor asked.

Uncle Robert nodded, the classic example of an intelligent buyer in Syria, who never showed too much interest.

The shop was a mixture of just about everything, from clothing to spices to pots to tapestries to games.

Masuda could see her uncle eyeing the vendor as he jiggled the change in his pocket, and she figured that the bargaining, which preceded each sale, was about to begin.

She stepped back to look at the backgammon set displayed on a table near where they had entered. Alternating turquoise and ivory stones made up the star shaped pattern on the box. It had the kind of beautiful craftsmanship that her father always appreciated.

Rabbi Shtern picked up a bundle of socks and turned to Uncle Robert.

"How much?" Uncle Robert asked the vendor, pointing to the socks.

Masuda lingered by the doorway for a moment before stepping outside the shop. She looked to the right, down the road as far as her eye could see, where the sandy haze blurred the outline of the horizon, so that her eye was unsure of where the sky ended and the earth began.

There, a building stood, blocking her full view of the horizon. Made of stone, she wondered why she had not noticed it when they first came and why she was now so compelled to take a closer look.

The dark red structure cast a shadow in the bright sky. Masuda took a few steps toward the building, not wandering far from her uncle, and safety. She could still hear his voice from inside the shop.

Suddenly, she stopped as if a hard wall stood between her and the building. The building was a church — a church with marble steps and an iron railing. A striking engraving marked the front wall. The sight raced her heart. There was something about that engraving that caused her to move closer. She tried to squint her eyes, focusing only on the engraving.

Just a little closer and she would be able to see it clearly. She glanced back to the shop. Although draped fabrics covered the entrance, she was sure her uncle would see her as soon as he stepped out of the shop.

She slowly and cautiously moved down the road. She could see the engraving more vividly now. It was an engraving of a woman, standing, with her hands under her chin, in prayer.

Hot springs of fear penetrated her thoughts. Suddenly, the bag of green squash in her hand felt heavy, and she struggled to keep it in her grip. This was the same engraving as the one on the ring. The pieces of the puzzle drew together as a vision of Jamil and the pitcher flashed before her. The black awkward eyes brought back the painted figure on the jug. That worn painting on the jug of the woman

standing with her hands under her chin also matched the one she stared dreadfully at now.

The image on the jug, the ring and the church were one and the same, coming from the same source. So it *was* a Christian symbol! That made sense since Mrs. Faraj and her family were Armenians and the Armenians were Christians, which also meant that the ring could not have belonged to the Muslim housekeeper. Then who? The question darted between her thoughts as she remembered how Rabbi Shtern had reappeared with his long coat, rushing down the stairs before she had discovered that the ring was gone. She tried to dismiss him from her mind. He was a rabbi! What would he want with the ring?

At that precise instant, with her mind in knots, the church bells rang, and two priests walked out. She stepped out of their sight. Even then, she could still see their white collars fastened around their necks with long chains hanging from them, their black robes brushing the road.

"Masuda!"

Her head snapped around. There, standing right behind her, were her uncle and Rabbi Shtern. She breathed in deeply, rubbing her eyes, trying to soothe the trembling that one could see just by looking at her. Forcing her feet to walk in her uncle's direction, she instructed herself to let out the breath stuck in her throat.

"What are you doing out here?" her uncle asked.

She looked at her uncle and at Rabbi Shtern and again at the engraving, unable to hide her thoughts. "I —"

Rabbi Shtern was silent. He gave her nothing to help her decide. Was she crazy thinking that he had anything to do with the ring? But it was this feeling. She had felt it before. It was a sensation that numbed her, trying to tell her something; an instinct growling inside, the same one that warned her to run from Jamil and his family.

"Sorry," she said, taking a deep breath, "I was tired and started to wander."

"Are you all right?" Uncle Robert asked.

"I'm fine."

As quickly as fear gripped her, her intuition turned into action and she reached for the small package in her uncle's hand. "Let me take this to Aunt Sarah. She's waiting."

"Why the rush? We will go together," Uncle Robert said.

"No, I insist," answered Masuda. "You don't need to waste your time and the rabbi's as well. I will take it for you. I know the way. Up the road and turn there," she said, pointing to the opening at the next intersection.

Uncle Robert smiled gently at her. "Alone?"

But she was already waving good-bye, on her way down the street. Panic drummed in her thoughts — the ring, the pitcher, the engraving. She had to find out. She had to be sure, she thought, running all the way back to her uncle's house.

CHAPTER TWENTY-TWO

*W*ITHOUT LOSING HER SPEED, SHE PUSHED OPEN THE front door. The housekeeper stepped out of the kitchen, almost tripping over her feet. "Yes, Miss Masuda?"

"Where is Aunt Sarah?" She swallowed, trying to quiet her heavy breathing.

"Gone," the housekeeper said, motioning outside with her hand.

"Gone?" Masuda stepped back.

"Yes, with Sion and Meir."

Now what? Instinctively, she turned around hoping to find some help, avoiding the fact that she was on her own. A picture of the ring flashed in her thoughts. Masuda ran up the stairs, two at a time. Rabbi Shtern slept in the other bedroom, adjacent to the bathroom. She stopped at the open doorway to his room and dashed toward the dresser drawers, before she could change her mind, hoping that her speed would give her the extra courage she needed.

The tall dresser was empty, except for a white shirt, an extra collar and some personal items that she pushed aside. The ring was too small. She would never find it. She ran her hand under the mattress. At home, that was her favorite hiding spot. But the rabbi knew that the housekeeper would be making the bed, leaving the mattress out as a possibility.

She had one other idea. Beside the bed was a small nightstand with a single drawer. Much more obvious than under the mattress, but it was her last chance. In there were his *tefillin*, enclosed in a soft case that filled the drawer. She slammed the drawer shut, disgusted at her suspicions. As she did that, something rattled around inside, but not like a ring; it sounded big and heavy, like a rock. She opened the drawer again, slowly this time, and removed the *tefillin*. Underneath it was a paper bag. She hesitantly looked inside. A small shiny black gun stared back at her. She squinted her eyes as she reached inside, wrapping her fingers around the weapon. She turned it from side to side, as if it would reveal some truth to her.

He carried a gun. So did her father. That didn't prove anything. She checked the barrel like she had seen her father do. There were bullets inside. It was loaded. But that still did not prove anything. When she put the gun back into the bag, it hit something, something small. She reached into the bag and could feel it. She slipped her finger inside and hooked it. There on her finger was the ring. The woman praying, just as she had seen on the church, right when the priests walked out, their white collars holding up their wrinkled necks.

White collar! She jumped off the floor and pulled open the drawer with the white shirt. Under it was a white collar. She held it up, bringing both ends together where the hooks met. He *was* a priest. The man whom everyone thought was a rabbi, that great tsadik, who prayed with two pairs of *tefillin*, was in fact a priest. A priest who pretended to be a rabbi all along!

Why would this man disguise himself as a rabbi? Did this have anything to do with her father? Then she almost chuckled at the idea of military officials from Baghdad hiring an Eastern European priest to find her father. What could be his motive then? In her mind, she sifted through every rational explanation, pushing away each idea as quickly as it came up, until she found herself in a very cold and insecure place.

Downstairs, the front gate slapped against the door-frame.

Masuda quickly stuffed the collar back into the dresser drawer. Aunt Sarah, she said to herself.

She gently closed the drawer and tiptoed into the hall. Standing at the top of the stairs, Masuda spotted the housekeeper dusting the bottom railing on the steps. It was not Aunt Sarah who had slammed the front gate. It was Rabbi Shtern, who was already inside the house, hanging up his coat.

Masuda quickly moved out of his view. He will probably want to go to his room, she feared. He said hello to the housekeeper and asked her for something in his broken Arabic.

Masuda calculated each step she took toward her bedroom. She quietly closed the door, hoping it would not creak as it sometimes did.

Without warning, panic cut through her as she pictured the way she had left his room. The dresser drawer she knew she closed, right after she had stuffed the collar back inside. But the gun and the ring were still on his bed. She was sure of it. But it was too late, too late to do anything about it. She could hear his heavy footsteps coming up the stairs.

Oh, why didn't she put everything back to at least cover her tracks? If he had not already figured out that Masuda knew he was a phony, he was going to find out very soon.

He was at the top of the stairs now. Masuda pressed herself against the wall, behind the door of her room. She was breathing so hard, she was sure that he could hear her. She was trapped. Hashem, she said to herself, please help me. Please!

Then she heard the bathroom door close and the lock fasten.

He didn't go into his room yet! He came up to use the bathroom. She opened her door and peeked into the hallway. The sound of running water pierced the quiet house. He would be opening that door any second, she thought.

Masuda flew down the stairs, maybe two or three at a time. She could hear the tinkering of the lock just before she flung open the front gate and leaped into the street.

Aunt Sarah. She couldn't have gone far. Masuda walked halfway down the street, and then stopped suddenly, turning in every direction. How far of a walk could she have taken with Sion and Meir? Masuda glanced at the houses that lined the street. Aunt Sarah sometimes visited with the neighbors. But who? Farhi, Zifrani, Serouya, they were all possibilities.

There was a nagging feeling, pinching at her senses. She could feel the source of her feeling coming at her, almost before she turned around.

Rabbi Shtern, or the priest, or whoever he was, was down the street, directly coming her way. Cold and expressionless, with his black coat flowing behind him, he was heading straight for her.

She looked around for one last sign of her aunt. Where *was* she?

Masuda caught herself as she tripped over a stone. Her hands grazed the ground. She looked behind her, judging the distance between them. What did he want from her?

Maybe he was angry. Then she stiffened at the image of terror that entered her thoughts. She pictured the gun, inside his coat, already cocked, and aimed directly at her.

The color black flashed behind her as she quickly turned the next corner at the rear of the grocery store. She gave up hope of finding Aunt Sarah. She had to think fast. The only one left was Uncle Robert. He was her last hope and most probably was at the *souk*. All she had to do was lose the priest long enough for her to catch the trolley. She would be there within ten minutes.

She ran, ran as fast as she could so that vendors and their customers peered at her flying skirts. All who noticed would say, "That is Robert Matalon's niece from Baghdad." And some would question her behavior. Under other circumstances, she might even explain herself. But her fear replaced all traces of shame.

Up ahead, she heard the trolley bells ring. Her heart leaped at her luck. Down the street, passengers boarded the trolley's yellow car. She caught up just as the last one entered.

Masuda looked around before pulling herself up the trolley steps. Just at it pulled away, "Rabbi Shtern" appeared down the street. He stared hard. She could not help but stare back. She would not show him her fears.

The trolley car slowed down as they entered the Old City of Aleppo. The driver called out the next stop. "*Souk!*" he said before slowing down.

Masuda stepped off the trolley. It seemed that almost everyone was going to the *souk* and she attached herself to a family of five, hoping to blend in with them.

She tried to remember which business her uncle was in. The tanners, silversmiths, jewelers, spice makers and tapestry vendors all looked unfamiliar. She could now feel the strange stares coming her way as she detached herself from the group. A single girl alone in the *souk* of Aleppo had many problems. But she had no choice. She kept moving, combing the kilometers of merchandise.

With no sign of Uncle Robert, she left the swearing and screaming sounds of the *souk* and began to straighten her thoughts. At least when she had left Dier al-Zor, she had had some sort of a plan that would bring her to her uncle. Now, her list of choices disappeared. Besides her uncle, whom else could she trust? She had no other family. Whom else did she know? And her father was arriving soon.

Her father! She was supposed to wait for him at Uncle Robert's. That was the plan. She had to return back there. But how could she?

She stood crying outside the *souk,* leaning momentarily against a cold wall made up of huge boulders. First she cried inside and then the sobbing seemed to take over and she was unable to control it. It wasn't supposed to be like this! Weren't things ever going to be right again? She stamped her foot hard with each step she took and felt the tears fall silently down her face.

The uneven old stones that lined the streets jarred her memory. Suddenly, a faraway but warm vision of the orphanage blanketed her thoughts. The orphanage! That was the answer. The Jewish Quarter stood up ahead as the only shelter in a sea of blackness. There, she would at least be safe, far out of his reach and far away from harm.

Chapter Twenty-Three

*I*NSIDE THE COURTYARD, SHADOWS COVERED THE HIGH walls of the orphanage. Near the front door of the stone building stood a *succah*, its wood panels streaked with dirt and its roof covered in rows of bamboo. Masuda stared at the wooden structure built especially for the holiday of Succot.[2] An opening in one of the walls served as a doorway. Old sheets hung on nails from the top of the walls, covering the inside completely. She couldn't help but smile at the handiwork of her friends, while remembering her father building a *succah* in their own courtyard.

She climbed the stairs and pulled a key out of the flowerpot. Then she took a deep breath as she turned the key and unlocked the door.

Masuda walked slowly down the hall, taking in the familiar sounds of a world she thought she would never be a part of again.

Children's voices rose from one of the open doors of the classrooms. Looking inside at the blank walls and dusty floors, Masuda yearned to become a part of this life again, surrounded by a comfort that does not come from money or prestige but from love and togetherness. All eyes were on her as soon as she stepped into the classroom.

"Masuda!"

She was not certain who called her name first, but soon they were all rushing to her side, crowding around.

"What are you doing here?"

"Masuda, did you come back to stay?" asked Tunie.

Morah Esther looked past her. "This is a surprise. Who brought you here?"

Masuda stood silent, a blushing color rushing to her cheeks.

"Masuda is here!"

She refused to offer any information about why she had returned to the orphanage and was thankful that Morah Esther was the one asking the questions. Morah Latifeh was out for the evening assisting her daughter, who had just given birth. Masuda was relieved at not having to face Morah Latifeh, and yet she missed the strength and honesty that emanated from the older woman.

After eating boiled lentils and steamed potatoes, the girls laughed and sang, preparing the rest of the decorations for their *succah*. Masuda remembered the last time she was here. Only a few days earlier, she had felt apart from them, as if she were the one giving to them, fulfilling a need in them. But now she realized that they were all in this together and that perhaps it was she who needed them most of all.

Before lights out, Morah Esther came to tuck her in, letting her know that she had taken the liberty of contacting her uncle and reminding her that they needed to talk, first thing in the morning. And Masuda thought, good, I will worry about it in the morning. Just as she closed her eyes, she began to go over the day's events. She thought of her aunt and uncle and realized how worried they must be. But sleep overcame her and she dozed off thinking about the morning. She would worry about it all in the morning.

CHAPTER TWENTY-FOUR

HE October sun glowed through the small window, warming her face. A moaning sound stirred her dreams. "Stop him. Stop him," the voice said, getting louder and closer. Instantly her eyes snapped open. In her dream, the image of the priest was clear, grinning, with the *Keter* in his hand. Horror enveloped her. But it was only a dream — one that raced her heart so fast that her breathing almost woke the others. Yesterday's conversation came alive. She remembered about Rabbi Shtern's hopes of duplicating the *Keter*. Instead, Uncle Robert had arranged to let him study it in private, today!

But she was away from all that now. She was safe. Nothing could bring her back there — except for news of her father's return.

She turned over and tried to fall back to sleep. But she kept thinking. It wasn't her fault that this man had come to Aleppo. If things were different, she would still be in Baghdad. Then it would have been someone else's problem. Someone else would have had to protect the *Keter* and let everyone know that Rabbi Shtern was a fake.

It was all so clear. But a little germ of honesty that hummed inside her said, "No!" She wasn't in Baghdad, Iraq. She was in Aleppo, Syria, and only she had discovered that he was a fake. If she didn't return to her uncle, then he might even steal the *Keter* for good, just like the many others Uncle

Robert had spoken of who had tried in the past. She worried about the safety of her little cousins, her aunt and uncle. How would she warn them?

She remembered the strange, wild look in Rabbi Shtern's eyes every time someone mentioned the *Keter*. Who else could know of his plan? The lives of her family could be in danger.

No matter how hard she tried, the idea kept coming back to her. And the harder she fought to push it away, the stronger it persevered, insisting that she live up to her responsibility. It was a responsibility marked with her name, and deep down she knew that as soon as she accepted that it was hers, it would come to her as easily as most of the things she accomplished that week — with her strong will and with the help of G-d.

Her final decision nudged her, pushing her to get up. She propped herself up on her hands. Everyone slept silently around her. What would they think if she left without saying good-bye? Well, it wouldn't be good-bye then. She would just have to come back, Masuda told herself as she threw off her blanket and wriggled her toes into her sandals. After washing, she took the *Tanach* her father had given her from her pocket and kissed it. For good luck, she told herself.

In the outdoor courtyard of the orphanage, Masuda yanked the handle of the metal door several times until it finally opened onto the street. Although the sun had just come up, the roads were quiet. It was time for her to concentrate. She cornered the tapered alleys of the Old Jewish Quarter and focused on a plan. Her fears narrowed on Rabbi Shtern. Sure she had to stop him, but how? He had a gun and it was loaded. The hard, cold bullets that filled the barrel of the gun stamped her worries. There was no way to stop him. Soon he would be on his way to the Great Synagogue to take the *Keter*. There was no doubt in her mind that his request to duplicate it was just a cover. If his plan was only to duplicate the *Keter*, why pose as a rabbi? What would be the point — unless his plan was not to duplicate the *Keter* at all. Taking the original was simply easier, not to mention the fact that the antiquity itself had its own priceless value.

She raced the sun to the Great Synagogue. Couldn't the sun at least slow down? That would give her more time to get there. Today was Erev Succot. Maybe the priest wasn't planning to spend the week of the holidays here at all. Maybe his real plan was to run with the *Keter*, today! This way, everyone would be busy with the holidays and their own preparations. No one would realize that it was gone until he was safe in Poland, or from wherever it was that he had come.

CHAPTER TWENTY-FIVE

*S*HE WAS GRATEFUL THAT THE GREAT SYNAGOGUE still stood shaded, not yet graced by the sun. Her feet hammered on the stones, the sounds echoing in and out of the countless arches. She sped past the outdoor *bimah* and pulled at the door to the front entrance. The tall door did not yield, remaining stiff and solid with each tug.

Locked? It was probably still early, she thought. But what if Uncle Robert and Rabbi Shtern were already on their way? What if Rabbi Shtern had already arrived, locking himself inside?

She stepped back, staring at the closed doors that shut out her hopes to save the *Keter*. Frustrated with herself, she dove for the door, banging with clenched fists. Someone had to hear her before Rabbi Shtern came.

"Please! Someone open!"

Suddenly the doors opened and the surprised *shamosh* bent his head in question. "Yes? Is that you, Masuda?"

"Oh, thank G-d! Mr. Attie!" Masuda tried to catch her breath. "Thank you so much. I have to explain. There is not much time," she said, looking behind her into the wide-open courtyard.

"Come, Masuda. Let's talk inside."

She nodded silently.

Masuda's eyes roamed the inside of the synagogue. It was dark and empty.

"Are you looking for someone? It is early. But a minyan[1] should be arriving soon."

"The *Keter*," Masuda asked, holding onto a bench. "Am I too late?"

"The *Keter*? What do you mean?"

"Has anyone taken it yet?"

"You mean Rabbi Shtern? He hasn't come, but we expect him soon, probably this morning, right after prayers. And he won't be taking it anywhere, just studying it in private, maybe in the smaller *bet midrash*."[2]

Masuda shook her head. "No, he can't. You mustn't let him." Worry swayed in her eyes.

"What do you mean? This has all been arranged. Certainly you know all this from your uncle."

"Yes, that is true, but …"

"What is it, child? You look frightened."

"He is not a rabbi."

"What are you talking about? Who is not a rabbi?"

"Rabbi Shtern. That is not even his name. I don't know what his name is."

"You are not making sense, Masuda."

Masuda took a deep breath. "He is not Jewish. He is a priest."

"*Shema Yisrael*! Are you certain?"

Masuda nodded.

"But how is that possible? I saw him myself."

"I know, so did I. He is a guest at my uncle's house. That is how I know. I found a gun along with all of his other things that priests wear."

"But how can you be sure that he is a priest? Maybe you misunderstood. Is it possible? Many people own a gun. And why are you telling me all this? Didn't you tell your uncle?"

---

1. **minyan** – (Hebrew) a group of ten men assembled for prayers.
2. **bet midrash** – (Hebrew) a house of study.

"I tried to find my uncle as soon as I found out … it's a long story. Mr. Attie, I don't mean to be rude, but there really is no time. I came here to warn you because I remembered that today is the day to remove the *Keter*. As far as I know, my uncle does not have any idea about this, and you are right. I may be completely wrong. But it is a chance that we must take. What is important is the *Keter*."

"Well, what would you like me to do? I am not the owner. I just work here, I open and I close. The decision will be up to your uncle and the other prominent businessman who holds the other key. There is not much I can do."

"You don't understand. My uncle doesn't suspect anything about the priest. He still thinks he is the righteous Rabbi Shtern. If they walk in here together, and we manage to tell my uncle, the priest may be armed and prepared to take the *Keter* by force."

The shamosh looked toward the Cave of Eliyahu. "You are right. It is better to be safe," he said, hurrying over.

"What will you do?" Masuda followed him.

"The only thing we can do. We must move the *Keter*."

"We?"

"It will be faster if you help."

Mr. Attie pulled a chair over to the ark in the Cave of Eliyahu, home of the *Keter*. Masuda did not even notice the smell of burning oil. Her eyes focused on the *shamosh*, who stood on a chair, opening the small door in the wall. She looked behind her. Hurry. Hurry, she said to herself.

Mr. Attie stood on the chair, pulling the heavy metal box out of the ark. Masuda reached for one end of the box. Mr. Attie's hand slipped, and the other end dropped down with a thud on the back of the chair.

"G-d forgive me," he said.

Masuda followed him, struggling to keep her fingertips under the edge of the box.

He grabbed the other end and they walked out of the

cave. "There are not many places to hide it. One of the other arks, perhaps."

"Won't they be looking there, in the other arks?"

"You might be right. That will be the first place. But where else?"

"Try somewhere simple, where they would never suspect," she said, her eyes probing the inside of the synagogue.

Suddenly, the doors to the synagogue creaked open.

"Someone's here," she whispered.

Together they clenched the box, frozen in their fear.

"Here," said Masuda, taking a step up to the platform used by the *hazzan*[1] for reciting prayers and reading from the *Sefer Torah*. "Up here on the *bimah*."

"No. He'll know."

"Not if we cover it. It will look good. He'll never know."

Voices echoed into the hallway, coming their way. Masuda hurled the box onto the *bimah* almost single-handedly. Quickly, they slid the box to the back of the *bimah* and pulled the red velvet cover over it. Masuda tucked a small part of the cover under the box to give the illusion of a platform. Against it, the *shamosh* stacked two piles of books and said, "G-d be with us."

Masuda stiffened as the voices sharpened, becoming clearer. She was certain now. It was her uncle and Rabbi Shtern. "I need to hide," she said, her voice quivering, looking for another way out.

"No one is going to hurt you."

"Maybe, but he knows that I suspect him." She turned around, starting toward the Cave of Eliyahu. Then she hesitated. That would be their first stop, to get the *Keter*. Her head swiveled feverishly seeking someplace — anyplace — to hide.

Instinctively, she slid across the floor, diving head first

---

1. **hazzan** – (Hebrew) cantor.

into the curtain hanging over the *heichal*, where the *Sifrei Torah* were kept. She struggled with the curtain and stood behind it, afraid to turn around to the holy scrolls just inches away. This was an audacity she had never dreamed of carrying out, standing between the holy scrolls and the curtain of the *heichal* that covered them. But it was permissible, wasn't it? Her life was at stake, she told herself. To save a life…she hoped G-d would understand.

CHAPTER TWENTY-SIX

"MASTER ATTIE!" SOMEONE CALLED, A VOICE SHE KNEW did not belong to her uncle.

"Greetings, Rabbi Shtern," he answered plainly.

Masuda aligned her eyes with the edge of the curtain.

"Erev Succot is not the time to start with business of the *Keter*, but my word is my word," she heard her uncle say.

"To fill the will of Hashem, there is no day too difficult. At any rate, we are not here to study the *Keter* in one day. Don't forget, I still haven't given up hope of duplicating the holy work," Rabbi Shtern said. He rubbed his hands together. "Let's take a look, shall we?"

A hush fell over the room and Masuda thought, good. That meant that Mr. Attie probably believed her and was going along with what they had planned.

In a snap the silence was broken.

"I'm afraid that is not possible," the shamosh said. "The *Keter* is not here."

"What do you mean, it is not here?" Rabbi Shtern asked.

"Mr. Attie, where is it?" Uncle Robert said.

The *shamosh* stood silent.

"Mr. Attie? Are you all right?"

"What is wrong with the man? Speak up!" the rabbi bellowed.

Masuda bit her lip so hard, it began to bleed. It was good that the *shamosh* wasn't cooperating, but at least he could say something, anything to deter their attacks. What if they badgered him enough to make him crack and tell them everything? She could not let that happen.

Masuda swung the curtain open.

The shocked faces turned her way.

"Masuda!" Uncle Robert said. "What are you doing?"

She shook off the looks of shame and insult. "It is not Mr. Attie's fault. He did the right thing!"

"Masuda, what are you talking about?"

"What is she doing here? This child is obviously playing games," Rabbi Shtern said.

Uncle Robert stepped beside her. "Morah Esther called me last night. She told me that you looked upset and asked that I wait until the afternoon to pick you up. Did you come here to look for me? Masuda, what is going on?"

Rabbi Shtern's presence seemed to weaken every bone in her body and she fought to stand up. Now as her uncle stood before her, questioning her, she felt the heat rush to her face and could not seem to find her words.

"Where is the *Keter*?" Uncle Robert asked plainly.

Masuda looked at the *shamosh*, who she knew struggled with the idea of lying to her uncle.

"Uncle Robert, I would like to speak to you privately, please," she said, eyeing the rabbi.

For the first time since they arrived, Rabbi Shtern stood quiet. "Excuse me," Uncle Robert said, leaving the rabbi with the *shamosh*.

Just outside the main sanctuary, Masuda spoke freely. "Uncle Robert, I know this may come as a surprise to you — a big surprise."

"Masuda, you look troubled, what is it? Has something happened to you? Is that why you ran away?"

"I don't know how to say this."

"Then just say it."

She looked down, avoiding her uncle's serious gaze. "Rabbi Shtern is not a rabbi."

"What do you mean, Rabbi Shtern is not a rabbi?"

"He's not even Jewish. He has a strange ring and a gun ... I saw for myself."

"I have a gun too. I'm still Jewish, aren't I?"

She stood in silence listening to the opposition she never thought to anticipate. He did not believe her.

"Where is the *Keter*?"

"I ..." How could she tell him where it was? Did she even have the right?

Uncle Robert left her and walked into the main sanctuary, walking straight up to the *shamosh*. "Do you know anything about this?"

Again, he did not answer.

"This is crazy!" Rabbi Shtern hollered.

Uncle Robert raised his voice. "Bear in mind, it is not just me who you will have to answer to, but to the entire congregation, for mishandling the holy *Keter*."

"It is my fault!" Masuda jumped in. "I made him do it. Uncle Robert, you have to believe me," she urged, peering at Rabbi Shtern.

"What are you trying to say? More nonsense? Where is the *Keter*?"

"Uncle Robert," her voice rose strong and clear, masking the trembling within her. "This man," she said, pointing to Rabbi Shtern, "is not a rabbi. He is a priest! In his dresser drawer you will find the truth. He is a fake and that is exactly why the *Keter* has been hidden — to be protected from him."

Everyone turned to Rabbi Shtern, whose eyes darted nervously from one face to the other. He stepped back slowly and shoved his hand into his coat, pulling out a gun.

Masuda gasped.

"Rabbi Shtern?" Uncle Robert called.

"Yes, I am a priest," he said, pointing the gun in their direction.

"Hashem have mercy. Masuda was right," Uncle Robert said before stepping slowly toward the priest. "Let's not do anything that we will regret."

"Uncle Robert! It is loaded!"

"No one is going to hurt you," Uncle Robert continued.

"Get back!" the priest yelled.

"*Shema Yisrael!*" the *shamosh* cried.

"You," the priest said, waving the gun at Uncle Robert, "are not a threat to me. I have come all the way to Aleppo for one thing. The *Keter* is my prize and I am not leaving here without it. Now tell me where it is before I shoot you all!" He banged his fist on the stone *bimah* just inches away from the *Keter*.

The *shamosh* wiped his brow nervously. Uncle Robert eyed Masuda. She stepped carefully to his side.

"Actually," the priest said, "it is better if I have you all together, where I can keep an eye on you." He stepped in closer. "Back up, all of you! Straight back into that cave over there. We are all going to take another look in that ark. I hope for your sake that we find the *Keter* there." Then he motioned to Masuda. "It would be a shame to lose such a fine young lady, once I start shooting."

The priest followed them into the Cave of Eliyahu, where he shoved Masuda and her uncle to the floor. Then he pointed to the *shamosh*. "You. Open the ark!"

Slowly, Mr. Attie opened the ark and put his hand inside. "Empty." He gulped.

"Where is it?" the priest screamed out in frustration. "I told you, I will shoot!"

Masuda looked at her uncle. He gave no sign to say anything. The *shamosh* was dripping with sweat, looking for direction as well. Her eyes started to twitch. Surely her uncle was planning something. The *shamosh* closed his eyes, silently moving his lips in prayer.

"Get up, you two," the priest said, barking at Masuda and her uncle. "Everyone against the wall, now!"

It was no coincidence, she thought, that he planned their death in the same place where many Jews had come for protection.

Her uncle glanced at the doorway, causing her to look up at a light shadow that inched toward them.

Was she imagining it? Was someone out there? Oh Hashem, please let it be true.

Suddenly a vision of a man passed before her eyes. He stood in the doorway, his strong shoulders towering over the priest.

Masuda's heart nearly stopped. Maybe it was just a mirage she was seeing, coming to tell her that her life was ending. She had heard of stories like that before — stories of angels or loved ones appearing to someone right before they departed.

But the image did not go away. It was her father! Suddenly, feelings of love and horror flooded into her heart.

The priest pointed the barrel of the gun directly at Masuda's head.

Then she saw it — a long iron bar, as her father raised it into the air. It struck the priest on the back of his neck. He shuddered and instantly slipped to the floor. The gun fell out of his hand and rolled to her feet.

Her father leaped over the priest and stepped on his hand before picking up the gun. Then he tucked it into the back of his pants.

"Father!" Masuda wrapped her arms around Jacob.

"Masuda!" Jacob hugged his daughter tight. "Thank you, Hashem," he said, his tears falling on her hair. He gently held her face in his hands. "Masuda, are you all right?"

Uncle Robert placed his hand firmly on his brother's shoulder. "Jacob, thank G-d you are here. If we would have

been here any longer —" he said, his voice cracking as he reached to hug his brother.

The *shamosh* shook his head, looking down at the priest.

"Mr. Attie, how about you?" asked Uncle Robert.

"How great are G-d's wonders," the shamosh said.

"How great are His wonders," they all repeated softly.

CHAPTER TWENTY-SEVEN

*T*HAT NIGHT, THE ENTIRE MATALON FAMILY SAT AROUND the table in the *succah*, under the light of the stars and the moon.

Sion and Meir jumped high to catch the candy that Jacob Matalon threw into the air.

"Jacob, it is good to have you with us," Uncle Robert said, looking admiringly at his older brother.

"It is good to be here," Jacob said. "Yes, Baghdad is a different place now. It is as if the entire country has shut down. General Bakr Sidqi has teamed up with Hikmat Sulayman to spread havoc throughout Iraq in order to overthrow the government. Prime Minister Yasin doesn't even have sufficient artillery to defend himself. Sulayman wants to be the next prime minister and it looks like he may succeed. King Ghazi just wants peace for Iraq. Even though the army has proved to be loyal to him, he may have no choice but to appoint Sulayman as prime minister just to control the snake," Jacob said, pounding his fist on the table.

Masuda sat back, listening to her father as the soft night breeze rolled across her face.

"It scares me to think of what would have happened if Shaprut hadn't rescued me from Sulayman's gang. But I understand that you, Robert, have had enough to deal with right here in Aleppo," Jacob added.

"It seems, brother, as if you came to our rescue just in time."

"They told me you would be at the synagogue. I went straight there," Jacob said.

"We have much to be thankful for this holiday," said Aunt Sarah, stroking Masuda's arm.

"What happened to the priest?" Masuda asked.

"The Syrian Authorities explained that he is wanted all over Europe for the theft of dozens of antiquities," Uncle Robert said. "He has connections with a black market that moves his treasures around the world before selling them for a lot of money. The value of the *Keter* is known all over the world. He was probably hoping to get a good price for it. But it is *he* who must pay the price. He is being escorted back to Europe as we speak."

"Was he really a priest?" Aunt Sarah asked.

"Yes, a priest who went bad, unfortunately."

"How did you find out about all this so quickly?" Jacob asked his brother.

"Well, our community's leaders have been quite persistent. French intelligence here finally told them that this phony was a priest in a small town in Poland. Apparently, he stole the funds that his community had set aside for needy people. He was on the run as soon as they found out and he has been running ever since. When he travels, he still poses as the priest of that poor parish in Poland. Only when he came to Aleppo to steal the *Keter* did he have the sense to disguise himself as a rabbi."

"So that's why he brought along his ring and his priest's collar," Masuda said. "I couldn't imagine why he didn't just leave them at home, instead of risking everything by bringing them along."

"That's just it," Uncle Robert said. "He wanders from place to place. His suitcase is his home. I was badly mistaken, brother." Uncle Robert rubbed his palm against his cheek. "G-d forgive me for letting this man into our lives. But your daughter knew better. She found out about him and hid the *Keter* before we even arrived at the synagogue."

"My daughter, huh?" Jacob smiled affectionately at Masuda. "You were the one in need of being saved and yet you saved us all."

More exhausted than anything, Masuda smiled.

"Thank G-d you are safe." Jacob softly pinched her chin with his fingertips.

When Masuda thought about it later, she realized that she had not done anything special. She only acted on a natural instinct — an instinct woven into the fine fabric of her soul. But she was not alone. She, along with everyone else who held the *Torah* dearly, was "keeper of the crown," wherever she may be.

GLOSSARY

batlawa – (Arabic) Syrian pastry.

Beit Hamikdash – (Hebrew) the Holy Temple.

bet midrash – (Hebrew) a house of study.

bimah – (Hebrew) a platform, usually raised, where the *Sefer Torah* is read.

Djamiliyeh – (Arabic) a town in Aleppo.

edjeh pataté – (Arabic) a fried pancake made from grated potatoes and onions.

Erev Succot – (Hebrew) the day preceding the holiday night of Succot.

fassoulyeh – (Arabic) bean stew.

fils – Iraqi currency circa 1935.

heichal – (Hebrew) the main ark where the Sifrei Torah are kept.

habbaz – (Arabic) baker.

hazzan – (Hebrew) cantor.

hohsh – (Arabic) a residence with an outdoor courtyard, usually walled on all sides.

kaffiyeh – (Arabic) an Arab headdress for men held in place by an *agal*.

kapparot – (Hebrew) the practice of offering the life of a fowl as a scapegoat, to atone for the sins of an individual. This Jewish ritual is done prior to Yom Kippur.

Keter Torah – (Hebrew) "Crown of the Torah"; also known as the Aleppo Codex. A Bible text on parchment kept in book form, with vowels and accents. The text was written and pointed by Aharon ben Moshe ben Asher in the 9th century, C.E. It is the oldest known reference for writing a *Sefer Torah* today.

kibbe – (Arabic) a fried torpedo made of cracked wheat and stuffed with meat.

Kiddush – (Hebrew) literally means "sanctifying." The prayers recited on the Shabbat meal.

kilo – 2.2 pounds.

kilometer – one thousand meters, 3,280.84 feet or .6214 miles.

kippah – (Hebrew) skullcap.

meter – a basic unit of measure in the metric system equal to 39.3701 inches or 3.25 feet.

mezuzah – (Hebrew) a box, fit with a small parchment scroll to hang on a doorpost.

minyan – (Hebrew) a group of ten men assembled for prayers.

nargeeleh – (Arabic) a water pipe with a flexible tube for smoking tobacco.

ner tamid – (Hebrew) eternal light.

Perashat Yom Kippur – (Hebrew) the Torah reading designated for the holiday of Yom Kippur.

Rosh Hashanah – (Hebrew) the Jewish New Year.

sefer – (Hebrew) book.

seuda – (Hebrew) meal

shamosh – (Hebrew) caretaker of a synagogue.

shohet – ritual slaughterer

siddurim – (Hebrew) prayer books

souk – (Arabic) a covered marketplace.

succah – (Hebrew) an outside structure used for dwelling on the holiday of Succot.

Succot – (Hebrew) the Jewish festival of harvest.

tahine – (Arabic) sesame seed paste.

Tanach – (Hebrew) the twenty-four books of the Bible.

tefillin – (Hebrew) a small leather box containing a parchment scroll. This is worn each morning for prayers.

Tehillim – (hebrew) psalms

tsadik – (Hebrew) a righteous man.

Yom Kippur – (Hebrew) the Day of Atonement.